The Elven Monarchy Scribes:

Book 3

New Found Legacy

H.L. Lafferty

Ladies
of the
Lakes
Publishing

Table of contents

~CHAPTER I~
STRATEGY

"Caspian. Guard The Banri's door. Communicate the situation to the healer. See if there is anything she can do if it is poison causing her ailments." The Princess fought within her mind, thinking there was a possibility this wasn't poison. "We need to figure out who is all devoted to Lyra within the kingdom."

"Your Highness, Zakarian was in the palace only days ago. It could very well have been him." Her trustworthy guard mentioned, his expression asking her to be realistic to the possibility that maybe Zakarian wasn't there just for her. He had a point. The Palace Guard had done an excessive amount of security checks and if any of the sorceress's minions were still here, it was surely a suicide mission. Alveen's anger grew as she thought of how the sorceress, her biological mother, had intentionally poisoned and successfully killed her close ally. She would keep killing, no matter who it was if she truly believed they could hold the portal open long enough to destroy all six kingdoms and the world along with it. One thought still troubled her with each new fact that came to light. After all the

● ● ●

kingdoms and this world were destroyed, where were the Dorcha tribe planning on going?

"You're right." The Banphrionsa let out a sigh of frustration. She was not accustomed to being tricked and confused. "Just relay the message to her healer and see if there is anything she can do to find out if that is indeed what is happening." Alveen turned to her niece. "Tanilly, you did wonderful. We will certainly have to increase your training soon." The Banphrionsa made sure to bend down to Tanilly's eye level. The more time she spent with her, the harder it was to believe how young she was. It was a delicate time and her connection and relationship with this young girl could have monumental ripples into the future. It was of the utmost importance that she continued to feed into Tanilly's actions and values. "Mysti is going to take you to my chamber. I'll meet you there when we're finished here." The young girl wrapped her arms around her aunt, giving her a quick embrace with a smile as she held Mysti's hand and retreated from the room. She stood about chest height on Alveen and her long blonde hair, straight as the trunks of pine trees, hung down passed her hips, swaying against her gown with every step. Alveen stood back up, returning to her professional demeanor.

"You have a daughter? Are you married?" Killian asked. Alveen was confused and shocked by the questions. She wasn't expecting them and her mind repeated the thought that it was none of his business if she was. He forfeited the right to be involved in her life. However, she needed to build even the smallest bit of trust if he was going to reveal everything she needed to know.

"No, I am simply mentoring her." She didn't make eye contact with him as she turned around and walked towards the throne created from manipulated branches and vines.

"She looks just like you."

"So, everyone keeps telling me." Alveen was frustrated and unsure what to do about her father in front of her. The last thing the kingdom needed was another potential threat running around. "Griffith." The guard snapped to attention, walking toward The Princess. "Take Killian back to the dungeon. Give him a clean cell, a more comfortable one if possible. Until we know his intentions, I don't want him roaming freely. Ruslan, assist him please." The guards escorted the chained former Prince out of the throne room, leaving Alveen to her thoughts. She sat on the smooth surfaced branches, resting her head in her hands, trying to find solutions to all the imminent threats that were now in play. Sitting back, she took a moment to enjoy the comfort of the throne. If the poison was caught before it was too late, The Banri would soon be back. Alveen was fine waiting for her chance to reign.

She waved her hand, summoning her fiancé for advice.

"What a beautiful surprise." Luka answered. It only took seconds for him to see the stress on her face.

"It worked. The stranger that came through the portal was my father, also known as Prince Killian."

● ● ●

"And?" King Luka had known her suspicions and had agreed that they were logical and very possible. It didn't surprise him one bit that she was right.

"And he had a lot of information."

"What's wrong Alveen?"

"King Hunter... he said he was sacrificed. He's dead." She managed to tell him through the catch in her throat and sniffling tears. She cleared her throat, composing her emotions quickly. "Apparently our theory was correct. With enough harvested moonlight and a strong enough sacrifice, they could transfer an entire kingdom to a different realm."

"We don't know if he's telling the truth though. This could be another part of her plan."

"What are the chances that she actually expected us to figure out the memory spell though? I don't think his placement is part of her plot. He said, and you could be right, he could be making this all up, but he said the reason she threw him through the portal and wiped his memory was more of an ironic torture, having him killed in his own kingdom by his own people, or in our case locked away since he wasn't murdered on site as she might have expected. He said that her goal, through all of this, is to get to me. To assassinate me. And he claims he refused to assist with any part of her plans that had anything to do with harming Zakarian or I."

"A lot of help that did Zakarian."

"He went of his own will though, that's not something he could have helped with. I just don't know if I should trust him."

"I wouldn't. Not yet. Where is he?"

"Back in a new cell."

"Good. Keep him there for a while. You can still go talk with him but you have enough to handle right now without him wandering around doing who knows what." She agreed, happy they were on the same page with her decisions. Though it was her kingdom, he would never tell her how to rule.

"Have you told anyone of our engagement?" she switched gears, going back to a less pressing matter. It was nice for her to focus on troubles that didn't end in life or death.

"I spoke to King Viktor. He wanted to tell me that his underwater guard found no remnants of Foresi. Did you know he and Willow had just gotten engaged as well?" Her eyes widened.

"No, I didn't. I would have thought she would have mentioned something like that."

"He said he was there the day before all of the disasters happened. I guess they had been courting in secret because they didn't want anyone to interfere. He's a worried mess as you can imagine." His facial expression hadn't changed. it was as if he were just talking about the weather. his eyes were focused on something else as they were talking, but she couldn't see what.

He seemed to always be multitasking. Alveen continued on the current topic, knowing that he was still able to hear her as well.

"Willow should be in the first realm. With all her citizens. According to Killian."

"But we can't get through to bring them back." He stated obviously, waiting for her to provide a solution.

"No. but he mentioned that there is a portal, in the syragon's lair. The sorceress keeps her sacrificial altar there, the more sacrifices she feeds it, the longer the portal remains open. Which will end up doing more damage to our world and closing the portal between ours and the first realm. He suggested that if the sacrifices were warded off for long enough that the portal will close and Foresi will return to its previous state."

"So, what are we supposed to do? Go charging into the syragon lair and fight off the entire Dorcha tribe and the sorceress herself for an unmentioned amount of time until the portal closes?" he asked with a tone suggesting she might be crazy.

"That might be exactly what we have to do." She paused rethinking what her options were at this point. "I need to see to Banri Vailion and her healer. Though I fear I know the answer, I am having the healer run tests to see if it is the life siphoning poison causing her rapid decline." His eyes of liquid gold met hers, hold their gaze for a moment.

"I love you." Luka whispered. Alveen blushed and couldn't help but smile, despite the morbid reality around her.

"I love you more." was her response. Luka only gave her a cocky grin and waved the connection away. Just in time it seemed as Caspian entered the throne room.

"Your Highness." Caspian approached her side, his expression stoic. His tone suggested that he had a serious matter to discuss.

"Yes Caspian?" Alveen stood looking at her guard and close confidant. One of the few in all Beannithe that she trusted.

"I wish to discuss possible battle strategy with you. Whether or not The Banri is indeed poisoned, this secret war must be ended before we lose more."

"I agree fully, however our first step must be to locate the constant moving lair that holds the sorceress's sacrificial altar. From my understanding there is a spell on it, linking the poison to it."

"Yes, we may have some scouts that can assist with that, assisted by your magic. However, Princess, I was thinking more battle ready. Since all of our kingdoms have been affected by this, I believe you should call upon your allies and request battalions of their soldiers be sent here to strategize, giving us a larger army to march upon the Dorcha with."

"Yes I intend on involving all kingdoms once we get to that point, but as I said, we don't even know where we're going yet, therefore we don't know where it would be best to convene. One step at a time, I will summon them all after I have spoken with Leigheas and determine our Queen's state." Caspian nodded with a fist over his heart symbolizing his respect for her decision. "If you wish to bring the scouts to the library, we can discuss how to find them from there."

Her dress flowed around her legs as she walked down the throne room stairs and out the metallic doors into the corridor. She pushed her shoulders back and stood tall. She would not be shaken. Now was the time to prove that Beannithe was right in branding her a genuine monarch. She would be aggressive and stop this war once and for all.

Alveen thrust the solid doors open as she passed the guards in her grandmother's corridor. From the doorway she could see her paling color and eerie lack of movement. Leigheas stood at her side, resting her chin in her hand, contemplating what to do next.

"Your Highness." She curtsied. Her short brown hair was messy and her face showed signs of exhaustion. She couldn't make eye contact with The Princess when she spoke. "I'm sorry. I've never run into this before. I have no idea what to do to help her." A tear rolled down her cheek but she still stared at The Queen. "She helped me so much and always treated me like a close friend. I hate that I can't do more right now. Her life literally depends on it."

"We are certain this is the poison that is affecting her?"

"Yes, I've run multiple tests to ensure I received accurate results. Every healing method I try, magic or non, it sucks it right out of her. I am able to prolong her life if I continue these things, but all it is doing is making her inevitable sacrifice that much stronger." The healer sat at the bedside, still looking deep in thought.

"I appreciate all you have done for her. I promise, should anything happen to her, you will still be welcome in the palace and treated as an old friend. But Sir Caspian and I have a battle to prepare for with hopes that these will not be Banri Vailion's last days." Alveen slowly turned and walked towards the door. Over her shoulder she spoke softly. "Leigheas, get some rest. There is a couch near the fire if you wish to stay in the chambers." Another citizen Alveen would trust with her life was Leigheas. She would be like a second set of security around The Banri while they planned and executed the battle to end the war.

The library was crowded with scouts and warriors. Apparently, Caspian had not made this meeting as exclusive as she would have desired. It was in his nature to be battle ready. This was an area of strength for him. As Alveen walked to the oversized table in front of the mantel, creatures knelt before her. She was taken aback by the vast display of respect. She looked to Caspian and he just smiled, following the others, kneeling before her. His hair was in its typical platinum blonde ponytail at the base of his neck, hanging over his leather shoulder holster that held his daggers. The hilts glistened as the flames from the oversized hearth reflected off of them.

"Whether you are Banri or not, you will find that you always have loyal followers out of plain sight." Her guard said with a small grin.

"I see that, but why?" A tall, lean warlock with short fiery hair spoke up to provide an answer.

"Banphrionsa, we have sat stagnant for far too long. The monarchs do nothing even when they are violently attacked at their core. We stand with you and your decision to pursue and eliminate the evil that divides our world. For all of those we've lost." Alveen looked around the room, creatures of all races and genders stood with her, willing to make a difference and take action. Willing to do something and be the change that no one else was willing to make.

"You might never understand how grateful I am for having such faithful and tough citizens." Sir Caspian stood next to her in front of the roaring fireplace that illuminated her citizens faces. "Our first step is needing to know where we are going. We are told they are constantly on the move, many times out of sight. I'm not sure how informed you all are but our goal is simple, eliminate as many Dorcha members as we can, and destroy the sorceress's sacrificial altar at the portal, defending the portal before any other sacrifices can be made." Alveen looked around the room making sure everyone was still following along. Expressions of patience stared back at her, waiting for more information and instruction. "Does anyone have any suggestions on how we find them? More specifically, how we find this portal and alter?" Murmuring followed with a low buzz of conversation as everyone was deep in thought and passing ideas around. Many ideas were suggested, but none that would guarantee locations.

"What if you did a portal location spell?" A small higher pitched voice spoke. On the second floor, Tanilly hung her head over the railing, her straight blond hair hanging over her shoulders.

"Tanilly. What are you doing here?"

"I was reading when everyone came in. It looked important so I stayed." She said innocently. Alveen shook her head but thought about what she recommended.

"Tanilly, is a portal location spell real? Is it possible to do?"

"Yeah, I read about it in one of these magic books." She walked out of sight and the crowd below could hear rustling of books and bumping on shelves as the little girl climbed to find the book she had already put away. Her quick steps echoed on the solid floor as she descended the stairs. "Here." She walked up to Alveen, placing a book in front of her. Caspian leaned over, reading the open page out loud with The Princess.

"You will get every portal that's accessible in Beannithe. So, you will see any portals into each kingdom that we already know about but it should surely show you any others, especially one that powerful." He spoke hopeful.

"That does seem like a good place to start." She looked to the crowd. "Does anyone have any other suggestions before we take this path?" No one spoke. "Alright. I will perform this spell and get us a location and I will contact our allies to seek reinforcements. I advise you all to begin preparing for battle. Train and find the best equipment. Caspian will keep you updated on our progress. If anyone has questions or suggestions, you will run them by him." She stood, waiting to see if anyone had any comments. "I suggest you spend much time with your families as well. We haven't the first idea what we are walking into. Dismissed." All the warriors stood tall and exited the knowledge filled room.

Alveen looked down to the little girl standing next to her, giving her a look that said she shouldn't have stayed in the library when an important meeting was going on.

"I did help though." She said with a big smile. Alveen couldn't argue with that. The spell hadn't been performed yet, they had a few things they needed to collect.

"If this works then I suppose I'll have to forgive you, won't I?" She asked with a chuckle. "Are you going to help me gather all the things necessary?" The powerful young girl nodded, walking out the door with the book and her guards trailing her.

Alveen sat proper in front of the fireplace, taking a deep breath. The other monarchs obviously saw reason not to fight, leaving her with little idea how this conversation would go. Taking a deep breath, she thought of all the monarchs and summoned them at once. A cloud formed for Foresi but as expected, no connection was made. The fog gave way to the familiar faces of Lovisa, Karolyn, Luka and Viktor. Lovisa and Viktor looked confused by the multiple connection summon she had created.

"Good afternoon everyone. I'm glad you were all available at the same time. I have a rather serious discussion I believe needs to be had." They all sat straight, giving her their attention.

"Alright Alveen, the floor is yours." Lovisa said ready to listen. Alveen first filled them in on the guest in their dungeon and the information she had been gaining to catch them up.

"Within the day I will be performing a locator spell on the portal keeping Foresi in the first world. Upon finding their location, my army is ready to advance upon them in an effort to destroy the sacrificial altar and keep the portal blocked long enough that another sacrifice cannot be made in order to allow Foresi to return and stop the natural chaos occurring in our world." She took a deep breath, waiting for someone to answer.

"That would mean a direct battle with the Dorcha, and possibly the sorceress herself." Viktor stated.

"Yes. Though it is not my main goal, I believe with as many of us as possible, we may be able to even put an end to this once and for all."

"You mean to kill the sorceress. Which you have also recently found out is your mother?" Lovisa asked. "Are you sure that's something you will be able to do?"

"I honestly don't know, but I know it is for the greater good. Our citizens shouldn't be afraid of travel and afraid of an attack or of the possibility and their families may not make it home at the end of the day. Security and safety is the least we should be able to provide for our citizens." They all contemplated. Lovisa being the first to reply.

"I will join you. Let us know where the locator tells you and we will meet you." She spoke confidently.

"Thank-you Queen Lovisa."

"I will not be able to join the fight, unfortunately there is simply too much to be managed here. However, I will send warriors to assist in your efforts, Princess." Karolyn spoke.

"I will be there, wherever you need me. For Willow. My army and I will fully support this rescue mission." Alveen thanked King Viktor, his obvious grief for missing Willow shown through. Everyone had known about the engagement by now.

"King Luka?" She asked professionally. He smiled at her.

"I will follow you anywhere, my dear." He said confidently. He had never been sweet in front of others, let alone the monarchs during a professional conversation.

"Do I sense that there is finally a courting happening between Bulgrakta and Cosaint?" Lovisa asked with a grin growing across her face.

"Indeed, Queen Lovisa. In fact, we've decided to step up and become engaged to ensure there will be no interference." Alveen couldn't believe he chose now to tell everyone this. She hadn't even spoke to her grandmother yet. No one knew in her circle of close friends yet either. She would have to tell them today.

"It's about time." King Viktor said with a small smile.

"I agree with Viktor. You've only been falling for each other since you met." Karolyn cut in.

"Yes, I suppose we have." Alveen said, not allowing the unexpected announcement to bother her. "Anyways, back to the subject at hand. I will contact you all once I've done the locator spell and relay my findings. Until then." She ended the connection only for the fog to immediately reappear, Luka wanting to speak with her privately.

"Hello beautiful. It's been so long." He chuckled with an expression that knew she couldn't stay mad at him.

"You could have at least informed me that you intended on telling them."

"I had no idea you were going to do a group summon! It seemed like as good a time as any since we may all be marching to our deaths soon. Someone may as well know of our status."

"I need to inform some of my confidants. The Banri doesn't know, but that may not matter soon."

"Is she still declining?"

"Yes. Leigheas is with her, prolonging her time. Every hour counts now. I'm going to do the locator spell. Prepare your warriors, King Luka. If this works, we go to war."

~Chapter II~
To End This War

Tanilly returned soon after with arms full of ingredients and tools that would need to be used to properly execute her task. Alveen assumed healers and witches had assisted with the list of necessities. Caspian and the scouts had joined as well, this time only a few rather than a room full.

"Your Highness, might I suggest using the royal study for more privacy." Caspian leaned in through the door with the scouts awaiting Alveen's answer.

"You're probably right. Best to keep this more private until we have a more detailed idea of how this will play out." She followed Caspian to a small door in The Banri's corridor. It looked like a closet door but upon crossing the threshold she saw a round table at the center, the top created from a slice of a large tree. The room matched the table shape with curved walls creating a circular room and walls covered with files and documents.

"Only few know of this room." Caspian confirmed for Alveen. "Much of these are legal documents for peace treaties, marriages and contracts between citizens. There are also journals every monarch has kept, going into detail about certain events and decisions." Alveen took in the room and the vast amounts of knowledge and wisdom surrounding her. She would have to look through it another time.

"This is perfect." The Princess spoke, leading her niece to the end of the table where Caspian had spread out a large map of Beannithe. "If they're in this world, we will find them." After mixing a small liquid bottle together of werewolf fur, a certain purple bioluminescent flower, the feather of a hippogriff, antler dust and palace bay water the concoction began to sparkle as each ingredient reacted with each other. Alveen looked over the spell book Tanilly had discovered, reading each line twice to ensure she knew what she needed to do. Tanilly reached into her pocket for the last piece needed. She handed over a clear harmonizing crystal to Alveen. The Princess laid the crystal over their location on the map and using a small dropper she placed ten drops of the now blue mixture on top. She closed the bottle with the mixture and stepped back. The droplets absorbed into the crystal but they could still see them from the outside, dancing around as if the inside of the crystal were liquid. The droplets began to shine as they expanded through the clear stone in front of the small group. The crystal began to vibrate, which was Alveen's cue to focus on what she wanted to find. She put all her focus on the portal and the alter. The crystal rose above the parchment map in a beam of light, leisurely spinning as it searched the map. The room had filled with a light blue glow as the crystal grew brighter. The crystal began to hover over open water, south of where Foresi was on the map. The light grew dimmer, pulsing gently with the crystal where it now hoovered upright in its position. They found it.

"There's no land there." Alveen stated. "They must be underwater."

"Look." Caspian pointed. The crystal moved at a snail's pace over the ocean. "They're on the move." Alveen slowly watched the path.

"They're moving north." She said.

"Directly towards the Foresi-Cosaint border."

"Caspian, I want the border shield enhanced. Make sure none of those creatures get through this time." She ordered her guard.

"Yes, Your Highness."

"I must reach out to our allies. We need reinforcements. Ruslan, prepare our warriors. I want as many as we can spare with us, but do not leave the palace or our citizens unprotected. We will have others with us." The guard bowed and jogged out of the secret room to carry out his order. "Griffith. Do everything in your power to keep her protected." She said referring to Tanilly.

"Of course, Your Highness." Alveen was left alone in the secret room with her newest addition to her guard, Stella. Alveen summoned her allies immediately, impatiently pacing as she waited for the connections to be made.

"Princess. What have we discovered?" Lovisa asked with concern. They all saw the urgency on Alveen's face.

"I need any warriors you are able to spare. They ascend towards our southern border underwater as we speak."

"My warriors are already prepared. We will leave immediately." Luka answered first, ending the connection after he spoke.

"As are mine, Princess Alveen. Though I will not be joining them I will dispatch those I can spare." Karolyn's connection ended.

"We will see you soon, Princess." Viktor said as he turned and broke connection.

"Alveen?" Lovisa asked. "Are you okay?"

"Yes. We can do this. End this sorceresses reign once and for all. We will get Foresi back and Princess Willow. We have to." She said in a stoic, controlled tone.

"You're right. We do have to be successful." Lovisa smiled. "Wear your arm cuff. It will help keep your mind clear. We will fly out within the hour." Lovisa ended connection.

"Princess?" Stella asked. "For what it's worth, for being only a temporary Queen, you are doing a fine job. I would stand behind you." With her fist over her heart she gave a deep bow. Though it was only a simple compliment, it made Alveen feel like this was the right choice. This was going to be successful.

After a while walking around the palace and informing guards and attendants of the procedures and events to follow, Alveen decided it best for her to head to her chambers for the evening and prepare for the next day. Her allies would arrive and they would be off to battle. This reminded her of her selflessness trial. The sorceress only wanted her, not all of the citizens. But this was not about her, this was about a greater goal to save everyone. Sleep fought her that night. Stella and Griffith guarded inside the room. Tanilly had stayed up for a little while reading but quickly fell asleep once the fire was roaring.

Alveen and Stella walked out to what was now the training grounds. The Palace Guard had taken over a field outside of the palace, over the last few weeks making it their own with a few sleeping quarters and an updated armory. Stella informed those in the armory that The Princess was in need of proper battle gear. After a few short minutes, lightweight armor was brought out along with holsters and weapons fit for someone her size. Caspian joined in carrying a small bag.

"Though I like to think I've trained you well enough that you don't need these, I have a feeling they will be needed." He handed her the small brown leather bag for her to examine the contents. Small potion bottles filled it. Alveen smiled at her mentor as she strapped on her thigh holster that held some of the potions she deemed most important and helpful. "Looks like Krumvite was full speed."

Alveen spun around to see King Viktor and his warriors walking up the trail toward the palace from the bay where two ships were now anchored.

"Princess."

"King Viktor. I cannot thank you enough for being so willing to join us." They hugged tightly before he answered.

"No, I can't thank you enough for having the courage to stand up and fight for our world. And for my Willow. We are all just as much in danger as Cosaint is. It is our duty to respond." He explained with emotion. Alveen couldn't imagine how much his heart had to ache.

"I heard about the engagement, congratulations. We will do everything we can to get her back and allow you a proper engagement party."

"I understand you are in need of one too?" He said with a sly smile. "Congratulations to you as well." Alveen bowed her head in gratitude, thanking him for his kind words. "And where is your fiancé' now?" Alveen stepped outside seeing the train cars had already landed on the outskirts of the training field. Warriors in black metal gracefully trained in the fields. Finally, she was the long black fur cape and the solid gold crown encapsulating her fiancé's handsome features. Her smile was unstoppable as he approached her. He tried to look tough and like the tough-to-the-core man that he was, but something about her broke his shell and he was unable to smile before he wrapped her in his towering frame.

"It appears he has been here a while." She said folding her arms as he approached. She turned to speak to Luka, "How long have you been here?"

"We arrived during the night. I told you I was leaving immediately."

"And you didn't even let me know of your arrival?"

"I assumed you would appreciate the sleep since you just preformed a pretty powerful spell. I was handling things out here. But I do apologize, Your Majesty." He smirked and he gave her a hug and a quick kiss on the cheek.

"Mmmm, I've missed you." She said with a smile.

"And I you." They parted and Alveen saw the looks on her guards faces who were standing beside her, as if they were blindsided.

"Oh. Um. I forgot to mention that King Luka and I are engaged now." Caspian smiled and responded.

"I knew it would happen." They all turned back to preparing the gear. Stella looked over The Princess and King, giving a glance of approval.

"We all knew it would happen. What I'm wondering is who broke first?" Lovisa asked with her arms crossed as she gracefully landed her alicorn. The field was soon filled with warriors sporting all different colors from their origin kingdoms. Luka didn't reply to Queen Lovisa's question.

"Eh, that would be me. I may or may not have allowed my excitement that we found a theory for this whole dilemma to effect my self-control." Alveen said quietly, slightly embarrassed by the admission. "But it turns out it was for the best." Luka rolled his eyes and began to walk away, but before he could, Viktor intervened.

"I actually brought something I believe will be of use to us." Viktor extended his arm, signaling a few bulky soldiers he had brought along to bring a large chest forward and another to bring a briefcase. He leaned down, opening the chest and pulling out one of the silver objects. "These are magically infused cuffs. They will give all of our warriors the ability to breath underwater, should that be where the fight takes us." He extended his arm, handing each of the royals one to examine themselves.

"Not a bad idea, but without these the battle might end sooner." Lovisa said.

"I'm hoping this battle won't be over until every one of them is defeated and my fiancé is returned along with her kingdom. These are to ensure that we have an even playing field, no matter where the fight goes. I advise everyone put them on under their armor so they cannot be ripped off." The royals could all tell that there was pain and worry in The King's voice.

"We'll get her back Viktor. We have to." He didn't nod in agreement or say anything to her. He just took a second to compose himself and acted as if he hadn't broken control.

"Alright, well Queen Karolyn sent her warriors with me so we are all here and prepared."

"Then we are off to battle." Alveen said as she climbed a tree, gracefully walking out on a branch to see all of the warriors that had come. Caspian blew into a loud horn, quieting the creatures in arms. She addressed them all now. "I cannot extend enough gratitude for you all being willing to fight for this world. As King Viktor told me, we are all in this together because all of our kingdoms and lives are currently in danger. The fate of our realm is resting on the success of this mission. King Viktor was kind enough to take the time to help us even the field and ensure the battle does not end before we say it does. Now that we are all here and prepared, we will travel together through the mountain range to the south. Before we depart, we ask that you all form a line and get a cuff from King Viktor. These cuffs, which you need to put on under your armor, will allow you to breath under water as there is a very good chance that is where we may need to go to complete our mission." Alveen looked over the creatures before her. None of them looked afraid. Despite her less than hopeful pep talk, she had instilled courage in them. "For Beannithe!" She yelled, receiving a strong chant in return. "Everyone grab a cuff and get to your mode of transportation. We will leave once everyone is fully equipped." Alveen climbed down the tree to meet Luka waiting at the bottom.

"What a blunt motivational speaker you are." Alveen just rolled her eyes, not allowing him to bother her.

"Would you like to come with me and check the location one last time?" She asked, walking towards the palace and not waiting for his answer. He followed anyways.

Luka was familiar with The Queen's Study. He had been in it once before during a council meeting. He looked around the room until his eyes landed on the glowing blue crystal hovering above the parchment map. "They're still not on land?" He asked.

"Well, the portal and alter are not on land. By the looks of the location, I would guess part of the tribe is spread throughout the mountains and the portal is underwater to protect it. I doubt they thought of the possibility of our armies being able to get to it. We best be on the lookout as we travel." She said. "I will have Griffith here to summon in case the location changes. He will be protecting Tanilly as well." She assured him.

"Thorough plan, Your Majesty." He said. Alveen glared at him.

● ● ●

36

"She is still alive and if we can help it, I will still only be a Princess at the end of this battle." She was not amused.

"I didn't mean to come off rude, Alveen. I just meant.." he paused considering his words, "The throne suites you. You have handled business so well and you were born to lead and solve problems. You care about not only your people, but all of our people. You will be a unique Queen." He held his hand out, ready to escort her back to their army. She glanced at him as if she did not want to accept, but she reached out anyways making him smile.

"Princess Alveen, is our course still set?" Lovisa asked as she approached her atop her silver alicorn, it's mane reflecting the late morning sun.

"Yes. I believe part of the tribe may be spread across the southern end of the mountains. The portal and alter are still now, no movement just off the coast of the border lake." She explained.

"We will inform the army. We will be on the lookout and prepared for battle at a moments notice." Lovisa had her hair tied in a tight braid off to the side and silver battle armor that fit her figure. Her clothing was durable and neutral colored and the leather of her tan boots rose above her knees. Though her outfit represented her, there was no doubt that she had her armor tested as Alveen's eyes stopped on the dings and scrapes sporadically indented. Lovisa yelled over the crowd as she rode through the army of mixed uniforms.

Luka had taken as many as he could in his cars since they would arrive the fastest. Viktor did the same on one of his ships, leaving the other in case his first was damaged beyond repair. Lovisa and Alveen led their warriors and the Loxlians via alicorn through the mountains. As they hit the barrier, Alveen hoped that Caspian had ensured it was reinforced as she requested. Alveen had on simple travel clothes with leather boots to protect her feet and leather cuffs for her thighs. Her armor formed to her abdomen and back, while the thick leather cuffs protected her upper arms, including the Krumvite and Irielle cuffs. A set of dark brown leather sleeves covered the top of her hands and her forearms, still allowing her wrists maneuverability. Her hair was pulled back into a simple ponytail that was pulled through the metal helmet she wore to cover her skull. Her armor was surprisingly lightweight, including the helmet, and she found she could still move with flexibility despite the layers. The afternoon sun was warm against the cool breeze as they flew through the border mountains.

"Below!" One of the Loxlian warriors shouted. Arrows began to fly into the sky out of nowhere.

"Shields!" Lovisa called. With the twist of the reigns, the alicorns armor extended over their soft stomachs and giant muscular legs. Their helmets extended down their necks and clicked into place with the rest of the armor, their necks still able to move with the thin layering of metal that no doubt had been designed in Loxley.

Alveen could see the cliffs edge, she knew they would be waiting for them, ready to ambush. But they weren't far now. "Lovisa!" Alveen pointed to her and ahead, then herself and down, motioning that they would split off, Lovisa taking her warriors on ahead and the Cosaintian warriors would handle the Dorcha below. She nodded in agreement. With a loud whistle Alveen pulled on the reigns, directing her army downward into the valley. Warriors whipped out their weapons, firing arrows as they saw enemies and blocking incoming fire with their impenetrable swords.

Allicent swooped in along the running stream below. As he gracefully landed, Alveen was off his back in a flash, allowing him to take flight again to get out of harm's way. Alveen pulled her hand-crafted daggers out of their holsters and prepared for the oncoming fight. This was the first time she had seen any Dorcha members, other than Zakarian and the syragons. They looked like her citizens, only tired and weak yet somehow, they fought aggressively like they were fueled by rage. Their blows were no match for an elf of her caliber. Her stealth, strength and speed blew through the small army in front of her.

Her warriors surrounded her, each fighting their own battles under the heavy canopy of the trees. Her feet sank in the sand along the edge of the stream as her newest opponent pushed her back with his persistent strikes. The leather of her battle-ready footwear protected her skin from the water but she

• • •

splashed and kicked it up with every movement. This creature in front of her was morphed as if his shoulders were dislocated and his knees unable to keep steady. It didn't make sense to her. How was such a body was able to perform such feats of strength and power. Alveen had no option but to use her own strengths. She reached her fingertips down toward the water, allowing it to climb through the air and into her palm. Once she had control of a small orb she released it with a focused aim into the face of the creature before her. She held it to his face, suffocating him. She would never get use to taking a life, but whatever was before her gave her and eerie feeling telling her something was very unnatural about him. The creature didn't scream or fight it. Through the orb of water wrapped around his head, he smiled. He didn't need to breath. Alveen took a step back as she was taken by surprise. She used her magic to manipulate the water into pushing her further downstream where she could recollect her thoughts and try to come up with a strategy. Caspian was at her side.

"How do these things die?" She asked looking at her mentor. He looked confused, with his brows pushed together.

"I've never had an issue killing them before. Maybe it's just the water?" He suggested quickly as he raised his sword to strike down the creature heading for them. Alveen stared, frustrated and angry at the creatures. She let out a frustrated scream causing her eyes to radiate that familiar white light. The creature before them, along with others standing near, burst into flames. She gasped, not expecting anything like that to happen. Was this her losing control again? She decided to make the most of it. She extended her arms quickly, twisting her wrists and fingers forcing the flames to chase after and swallow the other Dorcha tribe members that were now scurrying away in fear.

"I meant to do that." She said to her confidant, giving her a look of worry.

"To do what? Create fire out of nothing? Something that is supposed to be even magically impossible?" He countered with disbelief.

"Nothing is impossible, Caspian." She said pulling her last bit of magic back into her core. Bonfires of malicious creatures were scattered across the forest floor. Her warriors slowly walked towards her. "Come on, we don't have much time. We are needed at the cliffside." She said to Caspian, hoping he would relay the message to the warriors. "Remember, our goal is destroying the sacrificial altar and shutting the portal. Even if that means we have to defend it until the last Dorcha member is dead." She hissed, making sure their minds were all in the right place as they entered the real battle.

With a sharp whistle the alicorns all flew back around, flying low and slow enough for their riders to pull themselves up onto their backs and bee line for the cliff side.

Pushing past all the towering trees, Alveen kept her eyes straight ahead. When the trees parted, the war scene below her was splattered with bloody corpses, both her own warriors and her enemies. Viktor flew towards her on the back of an Alicorn he must have borrowed from another tribe.

"Princess! My guards found the portal. We need you." Alveen gave a sigh of relief that at least they had some advantage and were getting closer. "Follow me." He gestured, speeding away over the cliffs edge and into the mist. Alveen stayed close on his tail as she watched Caspian join the fight on the ground. Luka was also on the ground. His fighting skills never compared to another royal, except herself of course. At least that was one person she knew she didn't have to worry about.

Dorcha tribe members were crawling up the cliffside with speed unlike that she had seen from them before. A reflex in her began to throw spears of electricity towards the adversaries before they could reach her warriors. Shrieks cried out as she flew past them all, now hanging on the side of the cliff, their bodies slowly turning to ash and blowing away. Viktor began to slow down and pulled back up.

"The surface is near. We will need to dive down. My guards await orders. You will still be able to speak to them." He explained pointing to the bracelet, making certain hers was still on. Once he confirmed it was, he stood on the back of his borrowed alicorn and dove into the depths. Alveen knew this was the only way to make the destruction stop. With a deep breath to relax herself, she stood on Allicent's back, petting his mane one last time before she pushed herself off and entered the sea.

She was surprised when her eyes didn't burn from the salinity of the surrounding water. It could be an effect of the bracelet or it may even be her heightened senses since she had not been in the water since her trials. The chill of the water encapsulated her. There was no warmth from the currents or sun in these rough seas. She knew her elven body would withstand the temperature though. As she looked around, she found Viktor and his guards waiting deeper down. She breathed in, learning to trust her equipment as she kicked forcefully and stroked through the water.

"Can you see it?" One of the guards asked The Princess. She looked around and saw nothing at first, but a second glance brought something to her attention. Much deeper down in the cliffside there was a light shining out of what looked like a tunnel or entrance. She did a double take and looked at the Krumvite and Cosaintian warriors around her.

"Well what are we waiting for?" Alveen said with confidence, even though her own may have been lacking a small amount at this point. An eerie ambiance enclosed them as they pushed through the murky, undisturbed water. She almost preferred that the sea would be tossing and thrashing just as it was above. Alveen looked around, paranoid for an oncoming attack. They had to know they were all there by now, why was this descent proving to be so easy?

As the thought crossed her mind she felt something wrapping around her leg, just in time to send a shock through it and see what was following her. The seaweed that grew along the underwater cliff side was being controlled and had somehow silently wrapped up some of her warriors. Viktor turned just in time to avoid one of the strands that intended on twisting around him. Alveen dove back towards the base of the plant, unsheathing her daggers and slicing pieces that threatened her. She needed to free her warriors first. The water began to pull her as the seaweed created a current, trying to pull her away from her men. This was not a time for daggers. You can only beat magic with magic. She focused and sent a shock through the water, focusing it on the root system of the slimy weeds that now wrapped around the mouths and arms of her soldiers. The shock carried further than she thought, reaching Viktor and the warriors. The weeds froze and sluggishly floated downward as if the life had gone from them. The warriors did not receive the full end of the shock. Most were able to free themselves without assistance. Viktor had received an injury from the trashing waters throwing him against the cliffside.

"Take him to the surface. You all go as well, this is not a battle for you." Alveen ordered the guards around her. As they ascended without question, Alveen looked to the light below and swam cautiously until she found herself staring into the entrance of the syragon's lair. With their backs to her, it was easy to see the dozen monsters guarding the portal. Studying the structure, she noticed a large flat stone between them and the portal, with a small hourglass on it.

She leaned in trying to study it and figure out what it was when a hand reached around her face and slammed her into the cliff. Unable to make a noise through the hand that muffled her voice, she tried to get a look at who or what she was against. Everything was dark though. She wasn't unconscious and she knew she wasn't dead. With the smallest sliver of her magic she drew light into her eyes, allowing her to send a small glow out and give her a visual. Caspian. She tried to ask what he thought he was doing but Caspian put a finger to his mouth to tell her she needed to be quiet. His metal wings had created a cocoon around them. After a moment Caspian let out a breath and uncovered her mouth.

"What in all of Beannithe do you think you are doing swimming in there alone?" He asked her with anger in his voice, but keeping his volume low. "Those guards never should have left you. Apparently, I need to be by your side during battles like such."

"What do you think you're doing? I could have handled it. What's with the whole wing shield?" She gestured her arms around to his capsule.

"When I release this shield, be ready to fight. Fast. Use your magic. There is no time for sword play." He said. She did not question him. Taking a breath in she sent trails of magic into her hands and gave Caspian a nod that she was ready. As his wings quickly unfurled, Alveen was met with more of her own army fighting a swarm of syragons. "They will hold them off out here. We need to get to that portal." Caspian explained, pushing her into the tunnel.

A smaller syragon swam towards her. They looked different underwater. Their legs had folded up and been replaced with a thick sharp scaled tail that thrusted from side to side. Alveen reached out, grabbing its throat, driving her magic to heat up its insides and burning it within seconds. The ashes floated away with the current as more came upon them. Thrusting her arms out she pinned them to the tunnel walls, keeping them there as they swam by. Caspian drove his sword into them as he past, allowing Alveen to focus her magic on the next assailant. Carcasses of the syragons floated out of the erie tunnel as Alveen and Caspian made it to the center. The tunnel came to an end. The algae covered rocks falling from their pathway gave way to a wide-open cave interior. The light from the portal shined on every ledge and rock inside. Alveen swam down to the portal, observing the hourglass she saw from the tunnel. The frame molded from metals was now tarnished from the water and salt. In the top swirled a white liquid, but in the bottom a dark red one dripped.

"This is how the poison works." She said to herself. Without a second to think, she grabbed hold of the hour glass intending on breaking it. As she called on her power to break through the glass, a force threw her against the rock where it just sat, holding her down. The hour glass flew into the stone wall, shattering as Alveen still poured her magic into it. A smile crossed her face before she turned to face her opponent.

"NO! You ridiculous abomination!" Swimming over her, Lyra dove for the broken pieces of her tool. Alveen never remembered standing in front of her mother before, but there was something sinister about her eyes. They did not glow as an elf 's did. They were dull, lifeless. Alveen smiled knowing she had managed to complete at least part of what she was trying to accomplish.

Syragons poured into the cave with Alveen's warriors on their tails, still ready to fight until this war was finished. Swords clashed and clouds of blood poured out of the Solas soldiers as a syragon would thrash open someone's armor or a sword would slice through a syragon tail. Alveen could do nothing from her pinned down position..

"No matter." Lyra was upright again, no longer trying to grab hold of the poison flowing from the shards of glass or collect her ancient instrument. Her hair looked dull somehow and her face had taken on a green hue. The term sea witch would have been more accurate based on her appearance. "You will be an even better sacrifice. And it will solve my problem once and for all."

Caspian saw the altercation and threw the body of his last opponent towards the sorceress. She was too focused on her prize in front of her to react and was knocked onto a ledge nearby, releasing Alveen from her hold. Alveen swam up, getting a better view of the situation. Alveen called upon the water around her, creating spears of ice that she launched one after another, trapping the sorceress.

It didn't take long for Lyra to break through the icy barrier. Though she was able to manipulate things, the power of sorceresses still paled around an elf surrounded by an element. Alveen didn't waste any time. Freezing the water around her, the sorceress froze in her place, unable to move.

"That is my magic! How dare you use it against me!" She yelled as she floated upward.

"This magic was never yours." Alveen replied. Alveen controlled the water, bringing Lyra back down to a level she could speak to her at. "I have done nothing wrong to you. You claim to hate me and want nothing to do with me...Yet I am the whole purpose of your life still. I suppose that is one motherly thing you have accomplished." Alveen held her hands out and thrust the current towards Lyra, crashing her into the wall causing a crack in her skull where blood now poured out. She laid unconscious.

"Alveen!" Caspian screamed through the battle going on behind her. Two syragons dove at her before she could react. Grabbing each arm and carrying her toward the portal. Alveen tried summoning her magic but nothing came. Just like what had happened in Krumvite before. Alveen looked around confused, panicking now that her power was gone.

"Don't even try." One of the slimy beasts whispered. What could possibly be blocking her magic now? She wore nothing with an inscription and had acquired nothing new that would have stopped her magic. She looked around and noticed the arms of the syragons. Carved into their fishy skin was the inscription of a magic barrier, just like the one in her mask and Viktor's crown. She had to break free of them. They swam her closer, forcing her down on the flat stone that she had come to realize was the sacrificial altar. Alveen would not let this be the end. She had so much to live for still. She had people she knew she could help, she could make a difference and she was going

● ● ●

to bring good into a world that was so tainted with evil. The spark inside her ignited. She wasn't sure how because they were still holding onto her, but she could feel the flame dancing in her chest and the only difference was now there was a wall, much like in the beginning of her training, that she had to break through. It was going to take more energy than she had exerted before, but she was confident that it would work

One of the monsters forced her head down into the stone below her. Her vision went blurry and she could taste the red liquid now pooling in her mouth and she was crushed with the power of the sorceress that now stood behind her. New question, how would she kill the sorceress? With her cheek against the cold stone, her eyes met Caspian's in the distance. His eyes filled with horror as if he were watching an execution.

"Caspian! Get everyone out of here. I will finish this!" The guard gave her a hesitant look. He did not want to follow her order and leave her alone, but he saw in her eyes that hint of a glow that showed she was about to drop her barrier and allow her magic to pour out which could mean danger and death for anyone near. He reluctantly motioned his arms and whistled, watching his warriors retreat past him while he watched his Princess fight selflessly. She smiled at him through the crushing power on her chest.

"You're foolish to think you can overpower me now." Lyra pushed her staff forward, holding her daughter to the ground. Alveen reached her hand out as if she were grasping for something that was clearly not there. She closed her hand, crushing the alter below her with her heightened power. With a deep breath in she pushed her barrier down. The cool sensation ran through her veins as her body filled with magic, ready to be released. The syragons felt it in her arms and watched as the wound on her head healed. They let go and backed up next to their leader. Lyra noticed her eyes glowing brighter as Alveen turned her face. Her smirk was replaced with disbelief. Alveen focused, creating a spherical shield surrounding the lair and her own body. Her whole body pulsed as the magic in her screamed to get out. She released her control and destruction was all that followed. As Alveen exhaled she felt the heat on her skin but had her shield to protect her from further injury like what happened so long ago. She fought to keep her exterior shield together, avoiding harming any of her own warriors that would still be in the water outside the lair. Before her eyes, it was like the night of her first syragon encounter. The sorceress and her minions were incinerated and washed away with the current. She struggled to get her barrier back up. With every ounce of control she had in her being, she pulled up the wall that kept her magic at bay.

She floated in the dark cave, alone, as it shook and stones began to crumble. The only light came from the portal that was still open. With the sacrificial altar no longer siphoning from a sacrifice, Alveen knew it would only be a matter of time before the portal closed. She felt a presence behind her. Pulling light from the portal into her palm she held it up to reveal her brother.

"You killed her. Your own mother." He said with grief in his voice and anger in his eyes.

"I did what I had to do for my people. I would not let my people live in a world like the one she had planned."

"You say we are the evil ones, but the damage you have now caused will only bring a reckoning upon those you thought you were protecting." He slipped back behind the cave walls, disappearing. Caspian entered only minutes after.

"Princess Alveen?" He called out before he spotted her.

"Caspian!" She said as she sat in front of the portal, patiently. "I thought I ordered you to leave! How were you not harmed?" He flashed his wings, now charred like black iron instead of the metallic silver that they once were.

"Your Highness. We must leave. This cave will not hold much longer." He insisted.

"I will protect us." She said with a smile. She felt refreshed now, not exhausted as she expected to be.

"She is dead I presume?" He asked, trying to sound sensitive.

"Yes." She answered emotionless. Though that woman may have given birth to her, she was never shown love or compassion and she had never had a connection to her. As far as she was concerned, she was the sorceress that threatened her own life and the lives of her tribe members. "But I have a feeling someone soon will take her place." She wasn't going to tell him about Zakarian. They would all find out soon enough, she was sure.

"Might I suggest we guard from afar? Once this portal closed, this is where Foresi will return." Caspian pointed out, emphasizing that they would be crushed by the very kingdom they were trying to save.

"No. I will not allow anyone the chance to keep this portal powered. I will get us out of here fast enough. I promise." She said with her arms folded, looking into the spinning vortex. It slowly began to shrink and fade.

"It's closing." Caspian gasped.

"The Banri. Her energy was not used towards a sacrifice. Her life force returned." Alveen exclaimed, unable to stop smiling. The vortex dwindled still. Alveen grabbed Caspian's arm and focused her magic on her palm and feet, thrusting them out of the cave and through the depths toward the surface. As if on command, the portal must have closed and the water began to disappear from below them. From where the kingdom was ripped out from the ocean floor, it slowly began to reappear. As they emerged from the water, Caspian hit his chest, unveiling his metallic wings and holding onto Alveen, ascending up the face of the cliff. Trees appeared, towering past Alveen and Caspian, appearing in their peripheral vision. Alveen held her excitement in until they got to safety. They tore past the edge of the cliff side, seeing the warriors and royals, spread out across the cliff side, admiring the kingdom being pieced together behind them. King Viktor's face was pure gratitude and with her sharp eyesight she could see the glisten of a tear on his cheek. They landed gracefully, watching with the warriors of Beannithe see their hard work paying off.

Streams began to flow through the returned woodlands, pouring out into the newly reformed lake. In the distance, alicorns flew over the surface of the canopy toward them with Willow at the frontline.

"She's back!" Viktor exclaimed as if it took him seeing her to believe it was possible. Cheering erupted from the warriors as the newly named Queen descended into the group of allies. She jumped off her alicorn before he landed, running to her fiancé and wrapping him in a warm embrace with a passionate kiss that was almost uncomfortable to watch. "You're back. Willow, I am so sorry.." She interrupted him with another kiss.

"There was nothing you could have done." Willow looked up at her fiancé. "I want to get married." She stated.

"We are getting married." King Viktor stated, confused by her statement.

"No. I mean right now. All of the allies are here.." She looked around. "Where is Queen Vailion and Queen Karolyn?"

"Vailion is recovering and Karolyn could not leave her kingdom. She did send her warriors to aid us though." Viktor answered.

"Okay, well most of our allies are here. Please? Viktor I didn't know if I would make it back or not or if I would ever see your face again. I want to marry you. That I am certain. We do not need a huge party. We just need us." She explained with her arms still wrapped around him. He smiled down at her.

"Then so be it." He agreed after a moment. Many of the surrounding ears heard and let out different cheers of excitement. "My head guard is actually able to do this for us." A slender creature with smooth pale blue skin and large dark eyes stepped through the crowd. "Nixum is trained to marry others."

"That will be perfect." Everyone stood together, allowing Willow and Viktor to stand at the head of the crowd with Nixum reciting traditional marriage vows. Willow's hair was a mess and her traditional green and brown clothes were tattered, but the look on her face couldn't compare to the most elaborate attire she could have chosen. Viktor still wore his armor, his face was smudged with dirt and his helmet hair blew in the wind coming off the border lake. Like Willow though, the happiness in his eyes made the genuine emotion so much stronger on that day.

Weddings on Beannithe were, even normally, nothing like the ones Earth had. Alveen had learned that rings were not a symbol of marriage here, flowers were not picked for decorations and there were no wedding parties. There were elegant gowns, though there was no specific color it had to be. Often there was a large party, and during the party the two getting married would be escorted to a site with only a few people to declare their love and loyalty to one another. There was often a handfasting, where their hands were tied together to symbolize unity. Alveen would get to plan all of this soon enough for herself.

As Willow and Viktor both declared themselves faithful to one another, cheers erupted from the warriors that filled the field and mountain side. Lovisa had summoned Karolyn so she could be apart of the celebration.

Many of the warriors and monarchs set up camp that evening. Luka and Alveen were sitting near a fire when the newlyweds joined them, Viktor speaking as they walked up.

"Alveen. She thought of all this. Her and Luka did so much research while everyone sat aside. We should have done more. You really have them to thank." Willow turned her head toward her best friend.

"Is that true?" She asked walking over to her.

"We did our fair share of digging to help the cause. And may have started a turning point in the war to make it happen." Willow pulled her in for a ferocious hug.

"I knew I could count on you." Alveen whispered into her ear a response,

"You can always count on me, Queen Willow." Willow tensed at the title. "I am so sorry for your loss. I wish we could have done more."

"How did you know?" Alveen still held her hand as she spoke.

"Remember the prisoner from the royal walk attack?" Willow shook her head waiting for the explanation, "The sorceress had wiped his memory and identity. Luka and I found a spell that made him remember who he was and everything he knew. It was Prince Killian."

"Your dad?" She asked shocked. Alveen nodded, confirming.

"He told us. He was quite hysterical about it, that was the only reason I believed him. He told us everything we needed to know to confirm our course of action today." Willow looked around at the royals and their armies. "What of the damage to Foresi? Your people?"

"Nothing. My citizens were not harmed and our kingdom remains intact, even through the transfer." She said somberly. Alveen could tell the moment she began talking that this experience would change the new Queen forever. Willow was resilient though. She was tough and she was a carefree spirit. Though it would hurt her for years and years to come, she would choose to move on and move past the violence.

"Alveen. The sorceress? What happened?" Lovisa butted in to ask. Everyone's attention turned back to her.

"Wait, you fought her?" Willow asked astonished.

"Yes. She is no more."

"We're free. We have accomplished what the monarchs before us tried to do." Lovisa proclaimed.

"I wouldn't celebrate just yet. Unfortunately, I fear a new ruler. Though their numbers have diminished, I do not believe this is over yet. We may have a time of peace, but I do not foresee it lasting." She answered, not wanting to give the kingdom's hope, just for it to be destroyed. "Zakarian and Malika are still out there. Unless someone claims to have different information. I saw Zakarian but was occupied with the portal and unable to get to him." Grunts and groans of disappointment echoed through the circle of monarchs. "But their ruler is gone. We have time to prepare before another battle is set before us."

~CHAPTER III~
THE BANRI

"We are grateful for the blood and hard work you have put into our return." Willow said walking over to hold Viktor's hand.

"If there is anything you need or anything we can do, please let us know." Alveen hugged her friend and pulled herself atop Allicent who had been standing nearby. "We're only a mountain range away." Alveen whistled for her warriors to prepare for departure.

"We do have some reconstruction that is needed but not anything that will justify outside assistance. I will let you know if that changes though." Willow confirmed, staring at her allies with a grateful heart.

"We will see each other at the engagement party soon, I'm sure." Luka stated, walking away with Alveen.

"We were already married. We don't need a.." Willow paused, realizing how close they were, "Wait. Engagement party as in..?" She pointed between the two of them with a great smile. "Are you engaged!?" She exclaimed with excitement.

"Yes, we are." Luka confirmed. Willow squealed.

"I cannot wait for this! How long have you been engaged? When did this happen? *How* did this happen?" She suggested.

"Only a little shorter than yourself. It just kind of happened on its own since we had spent so much time together." Alveen tried explaining.

"She was seduced during long hours of studying and reading." Luka tried to be playful and funny. Willow couldn't help but smile and laugh.

"That sounds exactly like something that would win her over. What I'm curious about is how she broke you of your silence." She responded.

"He's never really been silent around me. I must just have something about me." The Princess blushed.

"You do have something very special and different about you." Luka whispered to her, kissing her cheek, making a dark red hue take over her face.

"Anyways.." Viktor broke up the sentimental talk, "We'll talk more about the wedding later. For now, we must all return home and celebrate this milestone with our citizens." Viktor instructed.

• • •

"We will see you soon, Princess Alveen. It's wonderful to have you back Queen Willow." Queen Lovisa said, hugging both of the girls. Alveen nodded. "I will summon Queen Karolyn to inform her of the progress we have made."

They all retreated to their forms of transportation, making off to their origin kingdoms. Luka had transported many of the centaurs from Cosaint, therefore followed them back since they would pass through anyways.

Alveen had never been so excited to see her village streets. As her and her warriors landed, there was no cheering. Sorrow filled the eyes and faces of her citizens. Masgo and his wife walked the main street. Alveen nudged her alicorn to speed up so she could ride beside them. Stella and Ruslan were beside her.

"Masgo! What happened here? We won."

"I fear you didn't. The Banri. She's gone." He said with tears streaming down his face. Stella and Ruslan gasped, looking at Alveen.

"She.." Alveen stumbled on her words. "she can't be gone. We broke the connection, she should be healing." Masgo just shrugged his shoulders. Alveen sped off towards the palace, riding him directly into the palace entry and through the corridors to The Banri's chambers. Staff members were walking out with blood covered towels and rags. Alveen's heart raced and her chest tightened. *No. no, no, no,* was all she could think. She hopped off Allicent, nearly falling to the ground as she tried to find the strength in her legs to see what happened.

As she stepped into the chamber, the scent of fresh blood swarmed her nostrils. Alveen couldn't feel her grandmother's presence anymore. She began falling to her knees when someone caught her. She didn't look to see who it was, she only began making small steps towards the bed. She could feel more than just this death here. Looking in the corner, Leigheas was being transported, her body limp with a fresh slice through her neck. Looking back at the scene before her, a tall blade impaled her grandmother where she had been sleeping and slowly recovering no doubt only hours before.

"What happened?" Alveen whispered in an attempt to not lose her self-control. Tears already streamed down her face, her chest was filled with a sorrowful scream that she knew she could not let escape. Sir Magnus walked up, his leg in a splint and his shirt sliced and drenched in blood.

"Malika, Your Majesty." He paused as she took in his words. "We were guarding outside and she just appeared in the corridor. She was full of fury that she took out on us. She seemed to have magical abilities, we were easily tossed aside. Leigheas tried to fight when she entered, but she was too swift." Alveen's face became red as the anger and hurt filled her body, weighing down her chest. She remembered to breath as she taught Tanilly to ensure no one else would get hurt by her lack of emotional control. "It was swift. She was recovering but she wasn't able to access enough magic or energy to fight her off." Alveen was shocked, her only family member that she knew for certain was on the side of right, was murdered.

"We did what we could. We succeeded at our mission. No one could have predicted this." The rough voice rumbled her body. It was only then that she realized it was King Luka that had caught her. Alveen spun around and wrapped her arms around him, burying her head in his chest. The fact that her death didn't serve as a sacrifice and they had accomplished what they set out to do did ease her ever so slightly. The fact remained that she was now dead though. Murdered out of frustration and rage, nothing more.

"Where is Tanilly?" She asked Sir Magnus.

"She and your attendant have been taken to your chambers and are under heavy security, Your Majesty, just as instructed." She had ordered them to watch over her. Luka reached down to hold Alveen's hand as she began walking out of the room to check on her niece.

"I trust this will be taken care of properly?" She asked with a shaking voice.

"Of course, Your Majesty." All she wanted to say was to stop calling her that, but the fact of the matter was that she was now the sole heir and reigning Queen of Cosaint. She locked her fingers around Luka's as they headed with their guards to her chamber. She squeezed tighter as the weigh of what all of this meant started to sink in.

Upon arrival, Tanilly ran to the door, being able to sense Alveen. Since they had communicated telepathically back in Bulgrakta, they had an odd sense of each other's presence.

"Alveen! Oh we were worried sick. We went on lock down for a while. What happened?" Mysti asked. Alveen thought on the walk there how to tell Tanilly. The only answer she came up with was to do it honestly. The young girl was too smart and Alveen could not risk losing her trust over something such as trying to protect her innocence. Because of who that little girl was, her life would be full of violence and war and she needed to understand the severity of that sooner rather than later. Alveen gave them a sorrow filled look, motioning to the couch by the roaring fire. The leaves outside her transparent balcony doors made the dreary day look more colorful, but the red simply reminded Alveen of the bloodshed.

"I have some terrible news and I think it best if you hear it from me." She said sitting on the chair with Luka hovering behind her supportively. "The Banri has been murdered." The ladies both gasped, Mysti covering her face to hide her shocked and hurt expression. Though The Banri was not her favorite, she had always been a kind and just ruler to them. Tanilly began to tear up but she kept her composure.

"It was my mom, wasn't it?" She asked, folding her lips in and closing her eyes shut tight as she tried to push her emotions back in.

"Let that out Tanilly, do not hold emotions in." Was Alveen's first response with a comforting rub to her back.

"How did you know?" Alveen asked as the young girl sat up straight, her cheeks now matching the pink tinge of her eyes.

"She was here. My mom. I felt her presence in the palace, so we hid." Tanilly looked at Mysti.

"Where did you hide?" Alveen asked.

"Here." Tanilly looked back and forth between Mysti, Alveen and Luka, unsure of how much to say. Mysti gave her a look that said Alveen would find out one way or another. With a sigh she continued. "I turned us invisible so she couldn't see us. She transported into the room so the guards were unaware, but after seeing the room empty, she left. But she had a mean glare on her face.. and blood on her pants." Tanilly said, hoping she would not get in trouble.

"You.." Alveen tried to comprehend her niece. Turning invisible was not an ability anyone of this world had possessed, at least not that she was aware. "You turned invisible?" She shook her head.

"Am I in trouble?" She asked.

"No, of course not. I've just never heard of anyone being able to do that before." Luka looked at her, unsure of how to respond. It was odd enough the girl had powers beyond what even Alveen was capable. "Stay here with Mysti." Alveen gave her niece a hug and a kiss atop her head before taking Luka's hand and heading out onto the balcony.

The season had chilled and the bright red hues were beginning to slowly faded to browns and tans, though Alveen was grateful for the occasional evergreen tree. The sky began to darken, revealing the stars and planets beyond their own, lighting the world in a new way.

"We need to inform the other monarchs of her passing." Luka agreed with a subtle nod. Alveen waved her hands, summoning all of the monarchs, with a cold breeze brushing her ponytail aside. Within a few minutes each of the monarchs were connected. After multiple of them asking why the need for a call like such Alveen finally decided to be blunt and to the point.

"The Banri was murdered. Not by the poison and obviously she was not taken as a sacrifice. Zakarian's lover returned from the tribe, impaling her." Alveen had swallowed any ounce of emotion she had in order to be able to contain herself during this conversation.

"I felt something was wrong." Lovisa commented. "Even though I felt so positive we had done our duties." She looked back at Alveen, "I am so sorry Alveen."

"It looks like we will need to have a double coronation." Karolyn stated, thinking about how Willow had never had a formal coronation.

"Actually, we held a small ceremony after my father's passing. So, it's unnecessary for myself. We also held a memorial. Since we had no idea when or if we would ever return." Willow explained.

"I believe we will just do a small ceremony within our own kingdom, after all, it won't be long before we will need to do two engagement parties." Alveen decided. She liked the idea of making it quick, simple and small and not making a big deal of it.

"We spoke about that." Viktor began, "I believe it would be best to do one large gathering since we will all be required to attend. It keeps Lovisa and Karolyn away for a shorter amount of time." He explained.

"We are perfectly fine with that. Where will we have it though? There are four kingdoms celebrating upcoming marriages." Willow intervened innocently.

"Honestly, Cosaint may be the easiest. It is central, weather is permittable and it is easy to travel to, unlike Bulgrakta and Krumvite." Karolyn suggested, analyzing each possibility along with the pros and cons to each kingdom hosting an extravagant event.

"I obviously have no objections, but what are your thoughts?" Alveen asked the other three. Luka shrugged his shoulders as if to say he didn't care where it was held.

"Fine by me." Willow and Viktor said in unison, giggling after at the fact. Alveen was not able to keep her emotions controlled much longer.

"Alright, we will be in touch then. Willow, I will contact you for ideas so I can get everything put together." She ended the connection without saying goodbye to anyone. The cool breeze had grown stronger, now able to push her tears to the side as they trailed down her cheek. Luka wrapped her in his arms, letting her feel the grief for he knew the consequences her magic would unveil if she bottled it up.

"I can do this." She whispered though she wasn't sure if it was meant for herself or for her fiancé.

"I know." He replied to the newly named Queen in his arms. "You are strong. Your instincts may have ended a war."

"Or started a new one based solely on vengeance and anger."

"Isn't that exactly what the last one was? Based on the foundation of pure hatred?" He smiled. "We haven't a clue what is to come." He paused, pulling her closer, "Except an engagement party and a wedding. Time to celebrate love and joy and prove that good will truly always outweigh the bad." She looked at him with disbelief. Her stoic King of the frozen tundra was melting on the inside and turning soft.

"Where is my realist fiancé?" she joked, giving him one final embrace before wiping her face and entering her chamber again.

"Your Majesty." Mysti curtsied, walking up to Alveen. Her heart still ached when anyone called her that. It would take a while to get used to.

"Yes?"

"We do need to get started on coronation and memorial plans. Some of the staff members wish to schedule a meeting with you to go over details." Alveen had forgotten how fast they did these things. Although it would be difficult, her grandmother deserved to be celebrated and at peace. She thought and came to the conclusion that there was no reason to wait. This meeting had to happen soon.

"You're right. When would they like to meet?" She asked unenthusiastically.

"As soon as possible."

"Alright. Let's gather them and do this before dinner." She stepped into the bathroom to attend to her makeup and assure she was presentable for this meeting. Luka had offered to go with her for support and to help with all the decisions. She accepted, knowing her brain may very well get overwhelmed planning two events.

The dining hall occupied about a dozen citizens that did much of the monarchy's event planning and staff members that would be helping out as well.

"Welcome everyone. I appreciate you all being prompt and prepared for these events. As you well know, I have never planned any of these events, therefore King Luka will be sitting in this meeting today to assist. You may begin whenever you're ready."

One by one each of the staff members and citizens asked her questions about decorations, invitations, set up, food, musicians and more. The planning had gone well past dinner. Alveen had ordered the palace to feed the staff and citizens working on the events that evening and Tanilly had joined for a short while.

"The Banri's memorial will be very similar to the memorial from the royal walk attack. Her body burned and her magic to rejoin the world again, strengthening our foundation." Luka explained.

"Is there any way to make both of these events happen on the same day? Perhaps we begin with the memorial, allowing allies and citizens to pay their respects and then do my coronation during the fireworks? This will keep her memorial lively and make it more of a celebration of her life and service to the kingdoms, but it will also be a respectful sign of progress in our lineage." Alveen explained, hoping that wasn't too different of a suggestion. They all looked around at each other. A fairy stood, speaking with a high-pitched voice. Her pink shirt matched her eyes and her black hair blended into her fitted pants.

"That is completely possible if you wish to celebrate this way. We were thinking of doing this as soon as possible. Within a few days, upon your approval, Your Majesty." Luka leaned in.

"That would be perfect for myself, I could spend a few days back in Bulgrakta attending to my duties there, and I can return for the celebration." He knew it was not his decision, but he wanted to give her some comfort in letting her know that was a good choice.

"I suppose there is no harm in that." She answered. "Is there anything else that needs to be decided?" She asked.

"Your attire, Your Majesty." One of the trolls mentioned.

"I will entrust that to my attendant Mysti. She has never allowed me to dress inappropriately for any event, I trust she will make sure I am properly clothed." They all nodded. "If that is all, then this meeting is dismissed. Please come to me if there is anything else that needs to be decided or if there are any issues." They all stood up and walked out of the dining hall. Luka stayed by her side.

"Are you ready for this?" He asked, squeezing her hand.

"For what? To become Queen?" She laughed. "Actually, I believe I am. I'm not nervous. I've been apparently doing a very well job the last couple weeks while The Banri was in recovery. I believe I will do well and excel in my new position." She explained with confidence. "But what do I do until then? I have a couple days."

"Since there is nothing pressing going on at this moment, you could work on planning our engagement party. That will have to happen eventually as well." He suggested.

"Another party. And then the wedding after that. Is it always this eventful?" She asked.

"Never actually. Between all the memorials, engagements, weddings and coronations, this is the busiest I believe it has ever been. And just think, Viktor and Willow eloped and we missed King Hunters memorial and Willows coronation." Alveen felt overwhelmed just thinking of how busy life was. "But, it will be a little while after the engagement party before we have the wedding, and after the wedding, there will be nothing for a while." Luka was right, Alveen thought. All that was left was a few events, she could get through it. After that, life would remain calm for a while.

It was only a matter of time before Zakarian tried to take back the throne or attacks yet again. She decided to enjoy the season of happiness until that time came.

~Chapter IV~
Coronation

"I said I wanted this small, quick and simple. There is no need to make a big deal of this. It should be more of a memorial for Queen Vailion, not a celebration for myself." Alveen spoke at the fog in front of her, frustrated that Luka had intervened from Bulgrakta, somehow able to make the simple transition of power into a grand party. Though it was still small, all of the allies were coming, himself included. It was beyond what she was planning.

"And it will be quick and simple. You were there for the other memorials. Why would you assume your allies do not want to be apart of Vailion's memorial and your coronation?" He asked, not understanding why she was so upset with him.

She didn't answer. Honestly, she didn't even know why she was so upset. Of course her allies would want to join her. Not only would they want to be there for her in her time of grief, but they would also want to be with her to celebrate this milestone in her life and marking the beginning of her reign.

"I'm sorry. I'm just overwhelmed I suppose. I will see you soon." She smiled, "I love you." He smiled at her.

"You better. I am awfully patient with you." He paused, "I love you too. I'll be on my way soon, My Queen." Waving the fog out of her vision, Mysti entered the room with a large garment bag.

"Oh no, not you too. Please tell me you did not go grand and extravagant." Alveen begged.

"Well, you did instruct me to assure you were dressed properly and appropriately for this event. Unfortunately for you, Your Majesty, that does mean extravagant." Mysti gave her a small smile, "But, I have a feeling you will love it." Her grin grew as she hung the hanger on the hook on Alveen's bed post. As Mysti unzipped the bag, Alveen could already see the shining fabric. When the gown was pulled out of the bag, Alveen stared, speechless for a moment.

The gown was meant to be fitted down her waist and over her hips, flaring out into a silvery satin waterfall at her mid thighs. The fabric was thick much like what she wore in Loxley, but it had an overlay of beading and embroidery. Each shoulder held a small cap sleeve, heavily beaded with crystals, that split into three straps each at her shoulders and criss crossed across her back attaching to the back of the gown.

"Mysti. This is magnificent." Alveen was lifting the fabric and admiring it.

"I told you you would love it. I made sure it was thick, now that we are in the cold season. And I also requested these for you. She handed her two boxes. Alveen sat on a chair in front of the fireplace, appreciating the heat warming her body.

Flipping open the first box she pulled out a large grey and black fur wrap with pockets for her hands. The blend of colors reminded her of large wolves back on Earth. It was beautiful and delicate and made her feel fierce when she held it. She set it aside and opened the second larger box. A pair of black boots, lined with the same grey fur to make sure she would be warm as she was outside during the event.

"These are perfect." She smiled, standing to hug her attendant and friend. "I knew I could trust you with this." Alveen pondered for a second. "Do you think I can trust you with another large project similar to this- not to be started yet?" She asked, thinking of an idea.

"Of course."

"I want you to be in charge of my wedding gown. I have a few details that I would like added in, but I believe you will know what will work best. Oh! And I will need a gown for our engagement party in the next month."

"I would be honored, Your Majesty!"

• • •

"Alright. Well I suppose I better get ready." Mysti helped her get in the gown and made sure all the back straps were properly lying to show off the crystals. After the gown was properly fitted and adjusted, Mysti went to work on Alveen's dramatic makeup, giving her smoky eyes of grey and black and dark red lipstick. Her hair was twisted and tied into an elegant and formal updo that would hold her crown in place.

Alveen asked to look the crown over. The silver crown had a thick band with clear crystals placed in delicate patterns that stood tall. She flipped it over, making sure she was not going to be placed under some kind of spell as Viktor was. No inscriptions. She handed it back to Mysti who eyed her curiously but knew better than to ask questions.

"Make certain this makes it to the throne room, please." Alveen instructed Mysti. She nodded and walked out the door with the box in hand.

"Your Majesty, King Luka approaches." Stella called into the room. Alveen had switched up her guards, wanting to keep her normal guards around her at all times, including at her door. Although there had been no news the last few days or any attacks, Alveen still felt as though something was going to happen and today was as good of a day as any. Her heart raced and her mind was on alert. Alveen approved the guards letting him in.

"Where is my.." Luka was speaking as he walked in the room. His look of stress and distraction melted as he saw her step out of the closet. "..beautiful wife-to-be.." He continued, looking her over. He loved the look of fur on her. "Have I ever told you how you remind me of an ice wolf?" He asked, kissing her hand. She gave him a curious glance.

"Is that a compliment?"

"It is indeed. They are beautiful, resilient, strong and they have the best instincts of any animals on Beannithe." He looked into her eyes, surrounded by precise dark makeup that enhanced her eyelashes. "They are also one of the deadliest, which I have witnessed you are capable of as well. You fight like them." Alveen wasn't sure what to say. She was certain she was blushing, but flirting back was not her strong suit. Normally she was witty and uninterested. As different as what he was saying was, she was loving every word. She was his ice wolf; strong and deadly and loyal.

"Shall we?" He held his elbow out to escort her to the throne room where the coronation would take place first. They turned down a few corridors and stopped outside the door.

"Are you nervous?" He asked, looking over her face for any hint of uncertainty. She glanced up at him with a smirk.

"Not even a little." He dropped her arm and walked in through the slightly ajar metallic doors, guarded as usual. Alveen stood in the hall, alone, while everyone took their seats and the finishing touches were made. It was a wonderful moment she had to herself, away from noise. She took a deep breath and shook slightly, preparing herself for her official announcement.

"Bow for Her Royal Highness, Banphrionsa Alveen of Cosaint." Upon the announcement, the guards opened the door, revealing the throne room filled with citizens. One step after another, Alveen found her way through the threshold. Though she tried to look straight ahead, she found it difficult not to admire the fact that even the second level balcony was filled with citizens. The pillars were swarmed with creatures of all kinds and the sun shined down through the roof, reflecting on the crystal chandeliers that hung in the midst of all the branches and vines. This site would have made many more nervous, but for her it simply solidified her confidence. She was born for this.

As she approached the stage where the throne sat, all the royals lined up, along with a handful of guards. Queen Willow stepped forward to begin the ceremony. She wore the typical formal attire of Foresi, her dark green gown with slits stretching high on her thighs showing the pants underneath, covered in holsters. Her brown leather vest over the simple material matched the boots covered in dim bronze buckles and zippers blending in with the durable material. The customary bronze crown sat on her short brunette hair.

"As a right of passage, all royal members are sent through The Monarchy Trials. An individual must pass these trials in order to receive the mark of a genuine monarch, meaning their intentions and character are deemed fit to rule by the realm itself. I stand here as a witness that Banphrionsa Alveen has conquered those trials and is ready to receive her promotion to Banri of Cosaint." Lovisa stepped forward next.

• • •

Her ensemble was more regal than the Foresian Queen's. The sky blue chiffon gown flowed around her legs as she addressed the citizens. The gown was modest with sheer lace sleeves and a high, solid neckline accented by the diamond necklace to match her tiara that rested on her knee length platinum blonde curls.

"I too, stand here as a witness to these events. For her to pass these trails means she holds strong the traits of a rightful ruler." Karolyn followed. The Loxlian Queen sported a knee length business professional dress, as one would expect. The black dress had short sleeves, a scoop neckline and a peplum at her natural waist, making it one of the more detailed dresses the Queen probably owned. She wore no jewelry other than a black and white watch that matched her heels, and a short silver crown with little detail.

"I stand here as a witness to The Banphrionsa's diplomatic growth and proof that she has solidified an alliance with Loxley before taking the throne." King Viktor stepped in line with the Queens. The men were in military uniforms as they often were at formal events. Viktor in a navy-blue suit with gold cords and Luka in his traditional black and gold. Viktor had pulled his black hair back into a small loose ponytail at the nape of his neck. His skin looked healthier since Willow had returned. The worry and stress gone from his eyes, even if it did take a toll on him.

"I stand here as a witness to The Banphrionsa's character. Not only does your future Queen have the ability to face evil and look beyond it to see the good, but she has more times than I care to count, shown her integrity and her choice to choose the right decision over the easy one. I also stand as proof that Cosaint and Krumvite hold an alliance as she takes the throne." He nodded his head as he made eyes contact with her. Luka was the last to speak.

"I stand here as a witness to The Banphrionsa's hard work and ethics. She has treated all with equal respect and stepped far out of her way to help others in need, even putting herself at risk to do so. I vouch for her selflessness, respect and hard-work that it takes to be a fit ruler of a kingdom. I stand here as proof that Cosaint and Bulgrakta have a mutually beneficial alliance as she takes the throne." Alveen smiled as he said his last sentence. To others it came off professional, but between them he was expressing his feelings of wanting a future with her as well. Lovisa stepped forward with the same crown she had looked over earlier. Tall and silver, rimmed with sparkling clear crystals.

"As The Elven Monarchy, we grant Her Royal Highness Alveen, the crown and throne of Cosaint." Gracefully, Lovisa lowered the crown onto Alveen's curls, making certain it was in place.

"Do you accept the duties bestowed upon you?" Queen Willow asked, standing at Lovisa's side.

"I accept the duties bestowed upon me." Alveen confirmed.

"Do you promise to protect your citizens and kingdom?" King Viktor continued.

"I promise to protect my citizens and kingdom."

"Do you accept the alliances moving forward and agree to maintain them as necessary?" Queen Karolyn spoke.

"I accept my alliances moving forward with all kingdoms and agree to maintain them as necessary." Luka stepped forward, holding his hand out, ready to lead her to the top step of the stage where the throne sat. As she accepted his hand, she couldn't believe the throne was actually passed on to her. She had been expecting Zakarian to bust through the doors or The Banri to be risen from the dead, but never did she expect there to be no complications.

Alveen took a seat on the smoothly carved throne accented with burgundy velvet for the occasion, running her hand along the branches and wood grain that made the back and arms.

"It is my greatest honor to present to the citizens of Cosaint, Her Majesty, Banri Alveen of Cosaint, The original kingdom of Beannithe." The citizens bowed respectfully towards their new Queen. Cheers and chanting rang through the throne room. Alveen couldn't help but let a small smile escape. Her citizens wanted her in this position, they thought she was a good queen.

"As you have all been made aware, we wish to continue this celebration with Banri Vailion's memorial out in the village. If you could all file out of the throne room, we will join you momentarily." Queen Karolyn spoke, instructing the citizens.

"You did well, Queen Alveen." Queen Willow spoke lightly as she approached her, giving her a dramatic bow.

"As did you, Your Majesty." Alveen followed suit, exaggerating her words and motions in jest. They spoke for a short while about Willow's coronation.

"Now for the difficult part." Lovisa pointed out after the citizens had filed out of the room. It was time for the memorial to begin. Everyone would be waiting outside. Alveen didn't have to give a speech but she wanted to say something before the official good bye to her grandmother.

Alveen found herself grateful for the fur wrap when she stepped outside. The snow fell heavily on the front lawn where Banri Vailion's body laid on a large log surrounded by leaves and flowers pulled to the surface by magic of course. Alveen stepped carefully over the frozen grass, being certain not to slip and embarrass herself. Luka stepped up beside her, wrapping his arm around her waist as an escort, but also because he could see how nervous she was. He knew she needed the extra visible moral support.

When they approached the log, Alveen looked over the citizens that gathers around. So many bright colors within the white snow around her. She had to admit she liked the funerals being this way rather the all black that she had become used to. Much like when Samual was burned, she did her best not to look at the body in order to keep her emotions in line.

"Banri Vailion reigned wisely. She carried peace and safety of her people near to her heart and I promise to you all I will do the same. May she join our ancestors." Alveen glanced at one of the fires going between the citizens, reaching out to draw a flame out from the pile and plunge it into the fire below her grandmother. She stepped back as everyone watched the memorial log quickly take flame and swallow their former Queen. Her body glowed and burst into the sparkling ash, floating away in the smoke high above them. As the cloud reached high enough in the sky, the royals extended their arms and fireworks displayed as the Queen's soul made its final exit.

"Now let us celebrate the reign of Vailion while sharing our excitement for the new Queen of Cosaint." Karolyn called out over the people. Many cheers erupted and people applauded in celebration.

Music began playing and citizens spoke amongst each other. Leaving the silence long behind them. Royals spread out among the citizens, celebrating the life of one Queen and the new reign of another.

~ CHAPTER V~
ENGAGEMENT PARTY

The gown Mysti had designed for the party was indescribably glamorous. As she often did, she made sure she dressed to match her loving fiancé. Her black sheath gown hung off her hips in a way that proved to be admirable without being provocative. Though the front fit her form nicely, the back adorned a train created from the same thick black material and golden organza with black applique. The v neckline was covered by golden glitter tulle that provided and overlay for the entire gown. A sheer material covered her chest and back, crawling with black applique embellished with golden accents. The material was heavy to protect her from the chill outside. A black fur wrap hung next to her gown, strands of golden glitter throughout the lush pelt. With her eyes made up in dark colors and shimmering tones, she put her boots on and went to her mirror. She was engaged. Midst all of the crazy events that had happened, it hadn't felt real until now.

"My Queen? Your fiancé awaits." Caspian spoke as he opened the door. Alveen took a deep breath and looked herself over one last time. "You look beautiful, Your Majesty." Caspian said as he waited for her to finish looking herself over. She threw him a glance of disbelief as she exited her chambers. She walked down the corridor with her hands clasped in front of her. Luka waited at the end of her hallway. As his eyes met hers, they traveled down her gown, taking in every detail. Alveen did the same to him. She noticed his slim fitting suit jacket and black dress pants with black polished boots. His hair was recently cut and styled over to one side. In his hand he held a blue thistle like the one he had left for her after the royal walk. She smiled at the memory of that blue flower.

"I truly am a lucky man, aren't I?" He said as she approached, leaning in to kiss her.

"And I must be the luckiest woman in all the realms." She added, taking his hand. He bowed handing her the flower. She grasped it in one hand before snapping the leaves and the stem to shorten it. He watched her to see what her plan was now. She reached up and tucked the flower securely in her hair that was pinned together in a low formal side bun. Luka tilted his head and looked her over.

"The perfect touch." He said. "You do look mesmerizing." He added.

"I will never fail to be impressed by how nicely you clean up yourself." She told him. "Are you ready for this?"

"A party where I am partially the center of attention and must make much small talk....Not particularly. You?"

"Same. Though I love the thought of our love being celebrated, I am not a fan of parties." She spoke honestly.

"And here I thought there was nothing that could make me love you more." He joked walking her out to the entryway. They waited to be announced patiently. They could hear the citizens laughing and enjoying the party already.

"Maybe they'll be too focused on the food and each other to want to talk to us?" Luka suggested hopefully.

"That would be desirable." Alveen admitted to him. She should have spoken up and said that they wanted something smaller but after the Foresi-Krumvite engagement and wedding being somewhat hidden, she felt like she owed a celebration to her people after the dark times that had just passed. The music stopped and together they heard them announce 'Her Majesty Queen Alveen of Cosaint and His Majesty, King Luka of Bulgrakta.' With a deep breath they both stepped forward.

Alveen and Luka walked out the palace entry to enter the party as they were announced. Alveen audibly gasped as she looked around. the ground outside the palace had been turned into an ice rink where citizens stood on skates, admiring the newly engaged couple. Icicles hung elegantly from the frosted over tree branches and vines that twisted in beautiful designs only to meet in the center of the ice rink and trickle down in a lush chandelier of crystals. Many were dressed in furs and black cloaks, making the scene before them more beautifully accented. Snow was falling from the sky above, silently landing in their hair.

"Now this is a party I can enjoy." Luka said taking a deep breath in of the icy air around them. The cold was most certainly his element. He turned and looked at his Queen. "Snow looks good on you. So does fur." He smiled.

"Are you saying I look the part of being a Bulgraktan Queen?" She asked with a mischievous smile.

"Without a doubt." As they reached the ice rink, Luka held onto Alveen's waist as they slowly slid across the ice to greet their citizens and friends. Only a few congratulated them at first and once the music started, everyone seemed to be distracted. Neither of them minded as they headed for the table of food that was laid out for people to eat as they pleased. They planned this to be a more casual event rather than a sit-down celebration that was customary.

Caspian had been patrolling the party, ready for any kind of attack since once again, all of the monarchs were together. There had been no disturbance in the kingdoms since the falling of the sorceress, but Caspian and Alveen had spoken multiple times. Both of their instincts agreed on one thing, that this war was not over. He walked up to Alveen, admiring his new Queen as she celebrated, though he could tell by her stance that she was not completely relaxed. She too was prepared.

"Will you escort me on a walk around the palace, Sir Caspian?" She asked, seeing he was walking near her. Now was as good of a time as any to ask him what she had been thinking about.

"Of course, Banri Alveen." He bowed with a fist over his heart.

"Thank-you. Crowds do overwhelm me. I just need to step away for a short while." He nodded in understanding as they walked down the path towards the bay.

"Banri, I must congratulate you on your engagement though I know I have before. You have found a suitable mate." Caspian spoke with a bow as Banri Alveen approached him.

"Yes, you have congratulated me multiple times now." She laughed. "I must give you some credit though. If you had not trusted him in the beginning and forced him to put forth the extra effort to prove his loyalty, I may not be in this position right now." The pebbles under their feet and shallow waves brushing against the shoreline created a background noise that helped ease the tension from Alveen's muscles from the worry of asking a huge favor of her mentor.

"You're welcome. I am glad you had someone you can trust. That is key in your new position. Finding those undoubtedly loyal to you." He said with a smile. He was genuinely happy for her, as a father would be for his daughter, though Caspian was not one to show emotion. The Queen started at him, her eyes reflecting the bright night sky and the golden ring glowing against her pupil. He lost his train of

• • •
89

thought for a moment. He had never seen eyes like hers, but they had that effect on everyone.

"I have been meaning to speak with you Caspian." She said, breaking his focus. "You are correct. In my new station I need to begin my search for those loyal, without question." Caspian shook his head. He would be a great asset for her since he was often on the inside of the citizens homes and businesses and worked within the guard. He would be able to help her find those loyal to her and those who defended her.

"I can begin the search. My eyes and ears are always open. I do know of a few that I would guarantee would defend you with their lives. Though they are not warriors." Alveen smiled, giving him a look that suggested she wanted to laugh at him. "What is it?" he asked, uncertain.

"I was meaning you, Sir Caspian." He froze mid-stride.

"Me?"

"Yes. I have come to view you as an asset, but by my side if you wish. I plan on filling positions of advisors in Cosaint since I will be between here and Bulgrakta after the wedding. You have proven your loyalty over and over again to me personally." Alveen explained with her hands clasped in front of her. Her loose curl blew away from her face with the evening breeze and as she waited for a response. The trail wrapped around the back side of the palace, through the woods. Though it was evening now, the moons and stars above lit the world alongside the bioluminescence.

"I don't know what to say. I.." He paused. Caspian, though he was Head of the Palace Guard now, he had never been an asset to anyone. He was always viewed as simply a guard.

"Just promise me you'll think about it. I would never wish to take you away from your Head Guard duties, but this would provide many opportunities for you to learn more and give you a greater title that you deserve."

"I would be honored, Your Majesty, I just..." Alveen's face froze, her gaze on something behind Caspian. The blood had run away from her face, leaving a pale expression in its place. "Your Majesty? Are you well?"   He asked reaching for her. Tears began to well up on the brim of her eyes and the teal and gold began to glow brighter as her emotions grew stronger.

"Caspian. Please tell me I am not seeing things. Please tell me you see what I see." Her hand covered her mouth. Caspian held onto her arm, making sure she would not fall. He turned around looking into the woods behind him. The bioluminescence had faded away only around the figure leaned against the tall evergreens. An emerald cloak hung over their shoulders with the hood covering the face of the stranger.

The intruder stood tall, facing them now, though the face was still covered by the shadow of the hood. Caspian could tell now that it was a man. Alveen's intensified senses certainly already identified the man.

● ● ●

"Reveal yourself, intruder." Caspian called out with authority. He was not at all intimidated, but something about this figure was terrifying his Queen. The man's jeans a dirty black button up shirt rang familiar in Caspian's mind. A gasp escaped his throat before the stranger's face was revealed. He knew exactly who this was.

"Is that really the way you would address an old friend, Caspian?" The familiar brown eyes buried into Alveen's heart as she leaned on Caspian for support.

"Caspian. Please tell me I'm not crazy. You see him, right?" She asked through tears.

"I see him, Your Majesty." Caspian looked back at the man. "How is this Samual? How are you here? We watched you die and burn." He spoke. Caspian was still confident as he spoke, even if he was baffled by the scene in front of him. Samual gave an evil grin.

"Your Majesty. How wonderful to see your radiant face again." He leaned against a large rock formation, closer to them now. Caspian nudged Alveen to step back. "I too have a new title." He stretched his arms out as if it appeared in front of him, "The Dark Prince." He smiled, but it was completely different than the smile Alveen had known and loved. There was something malicious in his eyes when he smiled.

"Prince?" Alveen asked, hardly able to speak.

"Your mother had quite a way with magic. Not the same as you obviously. Made me part of her plan before I could even say no."

"You were part of this all along?" Alveen asked. She was stepping in front of Caspian, who stood protectively at her side. Her sorrow, hope and love turned into rage, pain and betrayal.

"No. Your stupid brother did betray me. I had no idea of the plan. Something in his blade made this resuscitation possible... or reincarnation. Not really sure what it is considering since I was a pile of ashes." He rambled. "Anyways, I'm not here to ruin your celebration. Enjoy the party while it lasts. Soon your happiness will come to an end."

"Why would you say that? I did nothing to you. I loved you, Samual. What lies did they feed you?" Alveen asked, pain lurching up from inside.

"They fed me the truth, Your Majesty. It didn't take you very long to find another man to court, did it? It's plain to see my death had very little effect on you." That pushed Alveen over the edge, Caspian could see it in her eyes. The glow intimidated even the dark prince standing before her, insulting her.

"How dare you!" She screamed, thrusting both of her arms out and squeezing. The force threw him back into a tree, holding him above the ground. He just smiled. "I mourned for you. I neglected duties for you. Luka had the decency to allow me that time to grieve before even speaking of anything more than an alliance. Do not speak as if I was unfaithful!" A laugh escaped his throat. There was something so infuriating about him now.

"Oh? Is that so? If you had such strong feelings for me then what was it that drew you to him? That he is a King? It was the crown wasn't it?" She squeezed her hands tighter together, making it difficult for him to speak. "You just couldn't stand the thought of losing your crown if you were with someone like me. Someone became power hungry, I think." Alveen had heard enough. All of the good and bad emotions mixed in her being in that moment. She loved Samual, but he died. She had grieved and mourned her loss of him. She didn't eat or sleep, did he miss that whole season of her life where his death damaged her ability to want to love again while he was off hiding with her enemies? She did not simply jump into bed with the first King that came along. This was not Samual. Not her Samual anyways. This was just another way the sorceress knew to strike close to her heart, to destroy her without even having to lift a finger herself. Her frustration got the best of her. Pulling her arms back, branches broke and hovered behind her. "You're going to kill me? But my love, I've only just returned. Could you really live with yourself knowing you were actually the one that murdered me?" Samual asked without breaking his confident smile. She would not listen to these lies. With a powerful push forward, the branches pierced into the demonic form of Samual. He stumbled backwards with a grunt. Her power should have surely knocked him on his back. He gasped for breath, but only for a second before he began to laugh. He pulled each branch out of his body, no blood covering the surface or dripping onto his skin. Alveen could hear the distant footsteps of others running to see what the noise and shaking from her magic was. They would be here soon and see what she was witnessing. Caspian still stood beside her.

"You're going to have to try harder than that Alveen."

"What are you?" Caspian asked, astonished. He had never fought a member of the Dorcha tribe that didn't bleed or that could withstand a force like what Alveen had thrust upon him.

"I'm your downfall." He stated as his eyes glossed over in pure white, just like that of a syragon. "Consider yourself warned. Enjoy every breath you take, for I plan on stealing the last one from your lungs." He looked at the oncoming people with frustration, his eyebrows pinched. His body turned to a funnel of ashes and disappeared.

"Alveen!" Guards ran to where the figure had disappeared, but Caspian knew he was gone now just as Zakarian had vanished before. Luka was in the group. It took only a moment of looking at Alveen to realize something was severely wrong. "What happened? We heard an eerie echo of snapping." *They must have heard the branches all breaking,* Alveen thought.

"We will speak of it after the party." She replied. Alveen took a deep breath and looked at Caspian. "I will meet you in the study after the party dissolves. Bring only yourself." She added to make sure a dozen scouts wouldn't fill the study, a sacred and not well-known place. Luka did not like the answer he was given, especially since he could sense how troubled she was, though the look of terror and anger in her eyes along with the tears rolling down her cheeks was not hidden. He held her hand, her grip tightened as if she were scared. He rubbed the back of her hand with his thumb, a tiny and gentle gesture to let her know he understood and would be patient. As they were all led back to the party, it seemed as though not many of the other party goers, including the other monarchs, were disturbed or even heard the disturbing noise from before. Music was loud and the dance floor was full of citizens from multiple kingdoms.

Alveen stood with Luka and Caspian the rest of the evening. Creatures would come up and congratulate them or begin a conversation. Alveen tried to stay focused and be present. Viktor and Willow received many congratulations on their wedding. The guards began to guide creatures to their homes and visiting guests to their chambers. The other royals approached them before they retreated to their own chambers.

"Queen Alveen. King Luka." They bowed keeping eyes contact with the other monarchs. It was Karolyn who spoke. "Would the two of you be open to hosting a meeting tomorrow of the royals? We need to discuss much, especially in regards to the marriages between kingdoms since the four of you are the last of your lines." Alveen and Luka swapped glances of approval.

"I see no reason we can't accommodate that. I trust you all know of the Queen's study?" Alveen had chosen not to move to the Queen's chambers yet. She preferred her room and her view. With so much changing, she wanted one thing to remain familiar. To think, some time ago none of this would have seemed familiar to her at all.

As the party came to an end, Luka escorted Alveen back to her chambers. With her arm holding the crook of his elbow, he could tell she was thinking of worrying matters as they entered the palace and leisurely passed through the arched walkways.

"You know we are going to be married, right?" He asked quietly, reaching for her hand and pulling her to face him.

"Yes? I'm pretty sure that's what that party was for. To celebrate our engagement to become married." She gave him a puzzled look.

"Then why is it that you insist on keeping things from me?" She was confused yet again. "I can feel it. There are things you are not telling me. What happened out there tonight?" the concern in his eyes was authentic. She wanted to share with him, the party had not been the right time though. It surprised her every time that he knew what was going on inside her head.

"You're right." She sighed, allowing her professional appearance to drop. "I simply wished not to take away from the enjoyment of our party, that was all. I do wish to speak with you though." She clasped onto his hand and led him through her door, checking to make sure no one else was around. People would find out eventually but she needed time to process the new development. Luka stared at her, expectantly. He was far more patient than she could ever be. "Samual has returned." She said at first, awaiting his reaction. Much like her, it took him a moment to process the news.

"How is that possible? We all saw him murdered. We watched his body burn and his soul move on." He asked. Alveen could sense his emotions becoming stronger. Jealousy threatened to pour out, though he contained it. Hearing it out loud made Alveen flinch. She had moved on from her feelings with Samual, but that didn't mean the pain had gone yet.

"I'm not sure. He was in the woods. It wasn't him though. He talked of how the Zakarian and Lyra had somehow done something to him so his body would reform and he would be alive. But I am telling you, it's not him."

"Samual was in the woods on the night of our engagement party?" He was still focused on the jealousy that formed inside of him, ignoring the fact that someone had been reformed after death.

"Yes, look past that please. They have created a monster out of him."

"And you are wanting to go save him and bring him back into your life?" Luka said bluntly. Alveen gave him a frustrated glare. How could he possibly think that she would want someone else over him? She stared at him for a moment, irritated. She couldn't stay mad at him though. She reached up, running her fingers through the soft, thick fur along his jawline that was groomed perfectly as always. He tensed slightly at the tender reaction to his anger. His golden eyes were burrowing into hers as she looked at him, his irises hardly showing in the darkness. He had grown as a person and a King so much within the time since they had met. As Lovisa had said, they brought out the best in each other. Samual never did that for her. Samual never made her feel as confident in herself as Luka had. Luka went out of his way to make her happy and to ensure he was always there for her. Luka stepped out of his comfort zone for her and did things he hadn't done for anyone else. He showed interest in the things she was interested in just because they made her smile. Luka also believed in her and her strengths. He did not feel the need to always run to her aid because he was confident that she would be able to handle things herself, but Alveen was certain he would be there in a moment notice if she ever needed him.

"No." She wanted to raise her voice and be so upset with him but she understood how he must feel and the last thing she wanted to do was dismiss any uncertainty in their relationship. "Dear…" She paused trying to figure out the best way to word her feelings. "I love you. Samual and I were never as far in our relationship as you and I are now. You are the perfect choice for me, no matter how much we may irritate or frustrate each other. I have chosen you. I am marrying you. Not some demonic version of a former boyfriend who threatened to tear apart everything that makes me happy." Luka's eyes shot up at the last part.

"He did what?" His pupils shrunk as he turned toward the roaring fire, allowing more light to warm his face.

"Oh, now you want to listen?" She rolled her eyes and kissed his cheek. "If you would please have trust and confidence that I only long for you, you would have heard me saying that it is not Samual. Some of his memories maybe, but his personality and his ideals and values have been manipulated or replaced as it seems."

"How is that possible?"

"I honestly haven't a clue. It sounds like something far too advanced for a sorceress." Luka pondered this without responding. "I wanted you to be prepared. I wish to bring this to the attention of the royals tomorrow. I wanted us to be on the same page when we walked into that meeting." He reached for her hand, places a gentle kiss upon the back of it.

"I can appreciate that." He pulled her down towards him so she now sat next to him in front of the fire. She brought her legs up laying them across his lap as she wrapped her arms around his bicep.

"You know I love you right?" She asked, staring at his face, watching his eyes as they reflected the flames before them. He turned and looked over her face like he was searching for something.

"Somebody has to. I'm pretty sure you're the only one that's strong enough for that." He said placing a kiss on her forehead. She reached up, wrapping her hand behind his neck and pulling him closer.

"That's how you kiss someone you claim to love?" She joked. His smile now echoed her own as his tough exterior melted away for a moment. He leaned into her, gently kissing her neck and progressing towards her lips. His hand traveled around her waist, pulling her closer to him as his lips became more aggressive against hers. She let out a quite sigh of approval as his lips traveled up her jawline and he whispered in her ear.

"That's all you get for now, My Queen." A deep rough laugh escaped him as he pulled away. Alveen stared at him for a second before kissing his cheek one more time.

"That's all?" She asked innocently.

"Until we're married, yes that is all you get. I told you. I'm not nearly as immoral as everyone assumed. I am nothing like those who came before me." He said referring to his father being known for his indecency.

"I never thought you were." She smiled, leaning against his arm again, enjoying the heat of the fire to warm her from the wintery party they had come from.

• • •

~CHAPTER VI~
LAST OF YOUR LINES

Lovisa stood and waved her arms around in a large horizontal circle, placing a shield around the study they had all joined in.

"We are now free to talk without fear of eavesdroppers." Alveen had not heard of anything that could do that. It impressed her still seeing all the things that could be intentionally done. She had become so accustom to her magic being instinctual and being used for defense. King Viktor stood to speak first. His short silver crown rested on his shaggy black hair that was neatly tucked behind his ears.

"We are meeting today to discuss defense and protection for our citizens and decide how to handle the kingdoms now." He paused. "Does anyone have any developments on the Dorcha or do they remain stagnant?"

Luka looked at Alveen, encouraging her to say something. Luka spoke up, which seemed to surprise them.

"We have no new intel on their whereabouts. They seem to be lying low for the time being. I strongly feel we will want to keep scouts on the move. We have seen what Zakarian and Malika are capable of, and now they've risen someone from the dead." Before Luka could finish, Viktor interrupted.

"They brought to life someone from the dead?" Technically, they all knew it was possible, but rising one would mean sacrificing another, and generally speaking that meant whoever preformed the transfer, often meaning the ritual was not finished. Something in King Viktor's eyes made Alveen think that he was hopeful that it was his father. She intervened before the conversation was taken too far off track.

"Yes. The sorceress somehow managed to reassemble Samual from his ashes, but his spirit is tainted. It is no longer him inside his body. It is a manipulated form of vengeance that will serve Zakarian and Malika." She confirmed to the royals who all leaned in, listening to her intently. "Luka is correct though. We cannot simply sit around and wait for them to attack us. They have grown stronger."

"But we cannot forget they are mourning and they have lost their leader. Even the Dorcha will need time to restructure their society and create a new balance." Queen Karolyn brought to attention. She was right. Even if they were all heartless, revenge-filled creatures, a lose like that would cause a large disruption in their balance. "My honest opinion is to wait until after the wedding. We will all have security here and we will ensure we are all prepared for any kind of attack at a moments notice. I feel as though we should hurry that along though, Your Majesties." She suggested looking between Queen Alveen and King Luka.

"I have to agree. Royal engagements are never very long and with the impending danger, you really should consider moving with haste as you plan and set a date." Lovisa added. She had a look of sympathy in her eyes, but Alveen could see that she was only suggesting it for the best. They had good reasons. Alveen and Luka had already proven themselves through many trials and stood side by side through many battles and life obstacles, what was waiting longer going to accomplish? Luka was already staring at Alveen when she looked over to him. He had a small smile on his face.

"Well?" He asked. "What are we waiting for?" He reached for her hand, placing a kiss on the top. Alveen took a deep breath.

"Let's do it." She said. She had only dreamed of her wedding since she was little, but who said they couldn't pull it together in a couple weeks.

"Well, now that's settled. On related grounds, we must make a unanimous decision about how kingdoms will be managed now that there will be two sets of monarchs, each the last of your lines." Karolyn continued. Normally there was at least another monarch that could take over ruling each kingdom, so the newlywed couple would stay in only one kingdom to reign together. "Any suggestions?"

"We could continue our rules. Each staying in his/her own kingdom and visiting as we often do. I have found it makes you appreciate your spouse more when you give them space and have to look forward to seeing them" Willow suggested.

"Or we could set up a trusted court of advisors to rule over each kingdom while the couple is away. Obviously, if need be, we could separate during times of need, but I feel going back and forth may be the best. That way there is an equal presence of both monarchs in both kingdoms." Alveen suggested. "I have seen many of you leave your kingdoms in the hands of your trusted advisors and the kingdom still thrives in your absence. As long as we choose wisely, this may be a way to make it all work without compromising any marriages or reigns." She suggested. Her and Luka had managed to grow closer through that process. Much of their time had been together, or talking when they were apart. They had never really been apart for more than a couple weeks at a time since they had met. Just enough to make them miss each other and have their own space without putting too much distance between them.

"Or we could do both? Whatever works for each kingdom. Either way we need to decide on trustworthy advisors for when the monarch of each kingdom is away. Cosaint is the only monarchy that has not set one." Viktor continued the suggestions. "Foresi and Krumvite can keep to the way we have managed thus far, and Cosaint and Bulgrakta can choose differently if it suits them. We will not jeopardize the stability of any kingdoms or of any marriages." All other kingdoms had already placed advisors for when they were away. Cosaint always had multiple heirs or monarchs to rule or The Banri had never left if that was not an option, leaving Cosaint with an empty court of advisors.

"I like that idea. Give everyone the option and let them choose and change if need be. And I do have multiple people in mind for my court."

"And who would that be?" Luka asked, irritability in his voice that she had not spoken to him prior about this.

"I wish for Sir Caspian to be at the head of the advisors. He has proven himself beyond reliable and trustworthy and has stood by my family, and most importantly myself, in times of need. He led many of our citizens during our recent reconstruction of the kingdom and he had more than once given me sound advice choosing the path of righteousness above all. He has integrity, strength, a pure heart and a loyal spirit." Alveen was certain of her choice to appoint Caspian so highly. After all, he was the only one she truly trusted.

"We will each speak with him, and upon approval, he shall receive the highest seat." Karolyn responded to Alveen's suggestion.

"There is no need for myself to speak with him. I have been around Sir Caspian long enough and closely enough to know that he has my approval as well." Luka added. He had a high respect for Caspian. The guard protected his Queen well. He even had Luka followed to ensure his loyalty and if he was a trustworthy companion for Alveen. He had overseen many training sessions, including taking on the training of guest warriors before the battle and anytime they visited. Luka had seen his loyalty to Queen Alveen since he had arrived and that was something he respected above all else. Karolyn continued.

"Very well. Then the four of us will each speak with him on our own terms and we will move forward from there. Alveen, is there any others you would like to recommend for the court?" She asked politely. Alveen thought for a moment of those she could trust and that had been faithful to her.

"Yes, actually I do. However, I wish for them to be ran by Sir Caspian as he is a wonderful judge of character and has the ability to find out much about people." She looked around, noticing they were waiting for the names. "Elias, he works in the stable. He took on a great deal of responsibility when I asked at a moments notice and has proved himself ever since. He is young but I believe he has great potential if Caspian agrees. And Masgo, he has gone out of his way multiple times and had a grateful and appreciative spirit. If he is willing and is approved, then I believe he would be a great fit." Alveen sat back, "However I wish to speak with them first, as I am not sure of their level of interest in something like this since they do have other positions currently. I have already spoke to Caspian before I knew this decision was going to be made. He is aware I want him for this position." They all nodded in approval, looking between each other.

"Very well. Then we will begin interviews today for willing candidates. You will need to speak with Elias and Masgo once this meeting is over." Karolyn instructed delicately. Alveen nodded in understanding. She glanced over at her fiancé sitting in the important meeting with her. He gave her a sideways stare and a crooked smile. She couldn't help but let her lips show the smallest grin in return. Focusing back on the meeting, another issue had to be brought to light.

"Scouts will be deployed through the valleys and we will keep ourselves on high alert until we speak again. Is there anything else we must discuss?" Viktor tried concluding the meeting.

"Actually, yes. There is something of important I wish to bring to attention and I am under the impression that my grandmother never spoke to any of you in regards to this issue." She took a deep breath. "There is an heir for Cosaint." Everyone's eyes widened.

"You have a child? With whom?" Lovisa asked stunned.

"We should expect as much from the Bulgraktan King, but you Alveen?" Luka stood fast, insulted by the Loxlian Queen. Alveen shot her hand out, holding Luka back with her magic.

"Karolyn. Apologize, NOW." Alveen roared. "You speak of things you have no proof of. How dare you make insults based upon rumors." Karolyn glared at Alveen, but only for a moment before she realized the young leader was right. Karolyn had nothing to go off of except Luka's father's behavior. "If you could all so kindly let me finish before you make assumptions. I do not have a child, but Zakarian does." Everyone let out a sigh. "However, it is nice to see the core of some of our allies." Karolyn tried looking as though she didn't regret her words, but her eyes were apologetic. "Zakarian and Malika had an ongoing relationship as many are aware. They shared a brief romantic evening before we were sent away and of that, a child was conceived."

"How were we not informed? Where is that child now?" Viktor asked, upset. Willow had stayed quiet watching all the while.

"It's that little girl you spend so much time with, isn't it? She stays in your chambers most nights." Willow said quietly. Her face reflected that it was rhetorical because she already knew the answer. "She looks just like you. I wondered what the deal was." Willow spoke with a smile.

"She is in your care then?" Karolyn asked.

"Yes. Her name is Tanilly. She was in the care of Vailion until the attack. She has since then been in my care. The day of the murder of Vailion, Malika tried searching to take Tanilly with her, but she hid. This girl has extraordinary powers already at her age. She does not wish to go with them, and she is the last heir we have."

"It is her child." Karolyn pointed out.

"She is also our Princess. Meaning we owe it to her to protect her and keep her safe and trained until the time comes that she is to reign."

"Whoa, whoa, whoa. She is not of full elven blood. What makes you think she will ever have a chance to reign or that she is a Princess?" Viktor interjected. Karolyn pointed to him in agreement.

"That is the true issue I wish to discuss. Given the recent loss of monarchs and the lack of heirs, we must look into the possibility to extending our monarchy in order to avoid inter breeding within the royal families in later generations."

"That's hardly possible. They cannot rule unless they pass the trials. Magic wielding is one of those trials." Lovisa pointed out without coming off as disgusted by the possibility. She had been quiet for the most part, listening to everyone's thoughts.

"That is possible if they are above fifty percent elven." Luka added. "Tanilly gets fifty percent from her father, but somewhere down the line, Malika's family had to have been born of an affair long ago, making Tanilly's genes over that threshold giving her the ability to yield magic." Lovisa spoke up next. She had been in deep thought and her brow pushed together as she analyzed the situation in front of her.

"You say she is powerful, but if she is not one hundred percent elven, how is it she possesses so much of that ability?" Everyone thought for a moment. Alveen thought of Samual

• • •

who was a very high percentage elven and possessed the ability to wield magic, but it was never anything near the power that Tanilly had possessed. Alveen was stumped. "I am not sure, but I am telling you I have witnessed with my own eyes the power this young girl holds within her and it rivals my own."

"With the girl aside, she does have a point. It will only be another generation or two before inbreeding becomes a very serious possibility. One which I am certain we are all against." Everyone nodded. "It was once possible to avoid that with everyone having so many offspring. I have a proposal." Willow suggested. She sat at the opposite end of the oval shaped table from Alveen, her feet crossed relaxing on the tabletop and her fingers intertwined over her abdomen as she thought of an idea to solve this problem. "What if we open the possibility to marrying outside royal families. Our ancestors had many affairs, unfortunately, but that opens up a whole lineage of creatures with elven blood in their veins that are so far removed from the royal bloodline that it couldn't cause any issues. BUT the rights of the heir are contingent on multiple aspects. One, a blood test is done to determine the percentage of elven blood, we will only open marriages to those who are at least fifty percent elven to ensure a high blood percentage. Two, the heir only gets rights if they have the magical ability giving them the power to go through the trials. And three, all full blood heirs will have higher rights and pure marriages will be encouraged." Everyone stared at her as if she had this idea sitting in her back pocket all along. None of the royals had any better ideas or any ideas that were as well thought out as this one seemed to be.

• • •

"I think that is a perfect place to begin, until the issue is revisited. We do not have to worry about this until any of the current children come of age anyways." Lovisa agreed with the guidelines laid out before them. "This means the first step to Tanilly having any rights is for blood works to be done to determine her genealogy."

"I understand. We will do what we must today." Alveen understood. Viktor looked around.

"Alright. Is there anything else that needs to be addressed?" He waited for someone to speak up. "Then Alveen and Luka, the wedding will be moved up. We will remain here throughout the day to conduct interviews on those you have recommended and then we will return for the wedding." He looked around at everyone in agreement and stood. Raising his hand, he twisted his wrist and the shield around them was lowered, allowing outside ears to listen in once again. Alveen sat back in her chair as the others walked out. Luka hadn't left yet. He stood behind his chair, leaning on the back staring at Alveen.

"Yes?" She asked wondering what he wanted. He gave her a slight smile before he spoke.

"We should adopt Tanilly." He said quietly. Alveen was taken aback by the sudden suggestion. It wasn't that she hadn't thought about it. Her and Luka had even briefly talked about it when she told him she couldn't have children. The idea of being a parent had never really crossed her mind though.

"I'm sorry, we should do what?" She asked, making sure she heard him clearly and that he could repeat himself confidently.

"We should adopt Tanilly." He sat back down and stared at her. "Think about it. You already raise her. She is over half elven already, making her meet those new standards. She is powerful enough to thrive in the trials. She looks just like you and comes from the same line. She is your family." Alveen agreed with all of those things.

"Are you sure you're ready for that? You realize if this is what we decide to do then we are better staying together, as a family. She never knew Zakarian as her father. You will be the first and only person she knows as a father figure. She needs to be with both of us. We can't do what Willow and Viktor suggest." Alveen began to get anxious as she thought of Luka being gone so often. She was pretty much raising her now, with the help of Mysti of course.

"I don't want what they are suggesting. I want us to do this our way. To be together and assign an advisor's court to handle things in our absence. We can travel back and forth between kingdoms. As a family. She will need training and you are the only elf even in the same realm that possesses the amount of power she does." Alveen stared at how excited Luka had seemed about this. She was hesitant but she wasn't sure what about. She wanted to be with Luka and with Tanilly. She wanted to marry Luka. She couldn't have children and this was the universe handing her one. She had nothing holding her back.

• • •

"Okay." She smiled, holding back tears of joy at the thought that she would have a family again. "If you're sure this is what you want." She asked one more time. He reached up, cupping her cheek in his hand.

"This is everything I want." He planted a strong kiss on her lips and then got up to leave. "You have multiple people to speak with. When we reconvene to discuss the advisors court, we will propose our adoption. And we need to get the blood work started on Tanilly." Alveen nodded, following him out of the door and ensuring it was locked. "I will see you later?" He asked rhetorically.

Alveen first went to her chamber to speak with Tanilly. When she crossed the threshold, she heard the young girls giggle and hadn't realized until now, how precious that sound was.

"Alveen! You have to see this!" The little girl focused and closed her eyes. Her palms started to glow and her feet lifted off the ground. She was levitating in the middle of the room and her hands were directing her as she moved. She was flying. Alveen stood there, speechless. It had to be from the fairy portion of her genetics.

"That is so wonderful! Did you just figure out you can do this? Does Ollahm Hilfyro know?" She questioned the tiny powerful crossbreed that flew across the room and landed in her arms. Anticipating the weight, Alveen caught her effortlessly.

● ● ●
115

"It is exciting. I've bene practicing on my own. No, we haven't been working on anything like this. He is still teaching me the guidelines since we've had so many breaks in between."

"Ah. How were your classes today?" She walked over to the couch in front of the fireplace and set down the young girl, prepared to have a very serious talk with her.

"They were boring. I miss being in classes with other kids. I did get to play with some of them today though."

"I know, sweetheart. But we need to ensure that you are learning exactly what you need to know and that it is sticking. I am very happy you still go out and play with them. Do you have any new friends?"

"A few." She said unamused. Alveen wasn't sure how to begin this conversation that would change so much of her life.

"Tanilly, do you mind if we have a very serious talk for a minute?" Tanilly looked at her confused.

"Isn't that what we were doing already?" A chuckle escaped Alveen's throat.

"I suppose you're right." She looked at Tanilly without saying anything for a second, "How would you feel about Myself and King Luka adopting you?" Alveen braced for rejection. She wasn't sure how Tanilly would feel about it.

"Really? You guys want to be my parents?" Tanilly asked, her face unreadable still.

"We would very much like that. And as we've discussed, we are the only family we have left. I feel it would be best to make us a more permanent family."

"You and Luka aren't even married yet."

"We know that. We will wait to finalize everything until after the wedding, it is a long process, unfortunately. It involves a lot of paperwork being processed in Loxley." Tanilly watched Alveen as she spoke and a moment later, a small smile graced her face.

"I would love that. You are already like a mom to me. You've been taking care of me for quite a while now."

"I'm so happy you're okay with this." Alveen reached over and squeezed her niece in a loving embrace. "Now, I have something else that you might not be as happy about."

"Oh no. What?"

"In our royal meeting today, I began petitioning for your rights. Since you are not one hundred percent elven, the current laws would not allow you to reign. However, as of now you are the last of the Cosaintian line. They agreed to change the laws slightly, but in order for your position to be solidified, we must do bloodwork to prove your elven genetics." Alveen explained.

"Oh.." The blond elven-fairy sat there twisting her fingers. "And I have to do it?"

"You don't have to. I believe that you should. I didn't want to rule either when I first arrived here. I wanted to just be normal and not have all these responsibilities."

"What changed your mind?"

"I found out I am really good at it. I'm very good at protecting my people. I found out I have this increased power that I wanted to use for good." Tanilly looked at her, unsure how she felt about this situation. Alveen couldn't help notice how much she had grown. She seemed to have grown faster than the average elven child. Her speech had developed marvelously and her vocabulary was growing by the day, but she was certain Ollahm Hilfyro was to blame for that. He was turning her into an intelligent young girl. It would be her birthday soon. She would be equivalent to an eight-year-old.

"What if I'm not good at it?"

"That's what Luka, myself and Hilfyro are here for. And Caspian among other guards who are loyal. We want you to succeed and we will help you get there. You will never be doing this alone." She rubbed her back, trying to comfort her. Alveen had thought about how she would reject being adopted, but hadn't really thought about her not wanting to be a Princess or Queen.

"Okay. I'll do it." Her smile was weak, like she wasn't sure if that was what she wanted.

"You have so much time to grow and learn, my dear. This isn't something that will happen within days." A knock came at the door. Alveen reached out and opened the door from across the room with her magic. Luka walked in.

"Any chance she is ready for the tests?" he asked quietly. Alveen looked at her, she nodded silently.

"Yep, come on in." Alveen turned back toward Tanilly. "Do you want to sit on my lap?" She asked her. The girl crawled across the couch and sat on her lap. Alveen wrapped on arm around her shoulders and pulled her close.

"This is one of our healers. She is just going to make a small cut on your hand, take a sample of blood and then we will heal you right back up." Tanilly nudged closer to Alveen, but held her hand out and looked away. The dark-haired healer walked over, looking to The Queen for permission. She was middle aged in her face, but she wore makeup and did her hair nicely. Her features gave away her witch ethnicity with her dark eyes. Alveen nodded granting it. The woman had a small knife that looked as if it were chiseled from stone. With a quick flick of her wrist, she made the incision, causing Tanilly to tense up and take a deep and fast breath in. Once the blood was in the vial, Alveen reached out to heal her hand, but the wound had already disappeared. Alveen looked at Luka, again confused by the power before her. She covered her hand quickly and acted like she was healing it so the woman who took the blood sample wouldn't see.

"How long will it take to get results back?" She asked, rubbing Tanilly's back. The witch was stirring up a potion to mix with the blood sample.

"It should only be a few minutes. Once this is combined with blood, it will turn colors. The colors will determine her genetics. White is elven, pink is fairy, red is werewolf and so on."

"What about her exact percentages?" Luka asked.

"That's this test here." She moved her hand over a piece of slate with a large chart on it. "A drop of her blood in each of these areas will give us exact accuracy. The chart will pull apart the DNA and place it where it belongs on this chart, giving us exact numbers." Luka nodded, pleased that there were multiple tests going on.

"Can I go play?" Tanilly asked after a few seconds.

"Of course." She said. "Luka, can you please send one of the guards with her?" He agreed and spoke to the guard at the threshold, instructing him to stay near her, but allowing her time to play. Alveen smiled her gratitude towards her fiancé.

It was down to only the three of them in the room waiting for the results. The first test began to glow and the witch sat forward, studying it. Many colors swirled in the glass jar, but none of them were white. When it finally settled the liquid had turned into silver, gold and teal glitter. The healer reached in and touched the sandy particles that now filled it.

"That is certainly interesting." The particles began to glow and slowly vanished, leaving no trace of it behind. She quickly turned to the chart. None of the sections on the chart were filled, but each place the samples touched, a glowing scorch mark was left. They all looked between each other.

"What does this mean?" Luka questioned, assuming the witch would at least know.

"It means she is not elf or fairy." She explained.

"So, what is she?" Alveen pushed further.

"Honestly, I have no idea. Her genetics show no markers of any creature that inhabits our world."

"How can that be though? She looks just like Alveen and she had the pink eyes of a fairy. And the power of both." Luka exclaimed. There was no way she was a new random species that just appeared out of nowhere.

"Forgive me, King Luka, but my tests are never wrong. I am telling you, she is a new species on her own. By the sounds of it, one far superior to your own." She began packing up her things and walked out the door without another word.

"Do you trust her?" Alveen asked.

"I do. She is actually my guard's healer. She comes with us everywhere. I'm surprised you haven't seen her before."

"Me too. Anyways, she will be confidential about this?"

"Of course. She is one of my highly loyal. You don't have anything to worry about." Alveen still wasn't convinced.

"What do we do? I mean this certainly explains how she is so powerful already and how she can do things that most elves cannot, but where does that leave us?"

"I'm not sure. We will have to just be honest with the other royals. If she is in fact superior to us, then she should have a right to the throne. But she is not elven, therefore based upon our recent discussion, she has no rights to the throne." Alveen was hopelessly confused. If this was Malika and Zakarian's child, how was she not elven or fairy? Did Beannithe have some undeniable plans for this young girl and somehow started a new race with this one girl?

"I will go crazy thinking of all of this. I need to speak with Elias and Masgo."

~CHAPTER VII~
DECIDING THE COURT

In the stables, Alveen found Elias dutifully tending to Remia and Cordelia. Looking over, she noticed that Allicent and Beastil had already been tended to today. She could feel Allicent's soft fur as she ran her hands over his neck. The teal in his wings shimmered as if he were just bathed. He gave a neigh of excitement, which startled Elias.

"Oh! Your Majesty! I apologize, I didn't hear you come in." He had dropped his head in a deep bow. His deep voice echoed through the stable rooms.

"No need to worry yourself, Elias. I came to speak with you. Do you have a moment?" His face looked unconvinced that he had nothing to worry about.

• • •

"Of course, Your Majesty. What is it you wish to speak with me about?" He stood with his hands clasped behind his back, though it looked like a difficult feat given his broad stature.

"I, first and foremost, would like to thank-you for stepping up and caring for our alicorns so well. All four of them, none the less."

"I have a soft spot for them, you could say. It is really no problem at all. A large promotion from where I was."

"Speaking of promotion. I have a position, I wish for you to fill. It is not mandatory, but I feel you would do well."

"And what might that position be?" He asked, crossing his arms across his chest, intrigued by what The Queen was saying.

"With King Luka and I getting married, I need to assign a court of advisors I trust and that I know are loyal. I wish for you to take a seat on that court." His eyes bulged from his face, obviously not expecting the offer placed before him. "You will still be able to continue doing your duties and have a life of your own, obviously. But while King Luka and I are away, you would convene with whoever else we assign to assist in making decisions in our absence." The confused expression on Elias's face looked as if it may be permanent. "What's wrong?" She asked wondering if she didn't explain it well enough.

"Why me? Of all the people in your kingdom, why me? I.. I'm a stable hand. What good would I be on an advisors court?" The expression never leaving his face.

"I believe you are loyal to myself and what I work towards. I also believe that you would be a wise voice to have, as a voice of the people. There are multiple others that are working class that I wish to have a seat on this court. I will have certain guards placed in the court as well and I will not be unreachable by any means. But for the every day running of the kingdom, I need people I trust. And if my alicorns like you as they do, then you must be a very trustworthy person."

"I don't know what to say."

"I would advise you think about it, but make your decision soon. The other royals will need to speak with you and agree that you are a good fit for the court, but they will come to you."

"You know what? I'll do it. You have done nothing but provide great opportunities for me. Werewolves don't have a very high station normally, so I would be honored to take a seat on your court and represent my species."

"Very well. I appreciate all the hard work you've done. I will let the others know. Expect them to be dropping by before the end of the day." He bowed as she turned to walk out, heading for her next citizen.

Finding her way to the cobblestone street, she went down a few buildings until she reached the familiar butcher

• • •

shop. The business had been recently cleaned and the wood had all been re-sanded and polished.

"Ah! Your Majesty! To what do we owe the pleasure?" Masgo stepped out from the back at the sound of the door opening. He looked healthy and strong, which surprised her for some reason.

"You're looking well Masgo, so is your shop. How is your wife doing?" She asked curious as to how her recovery had gone.

"Alive and well, thanks to you of course. She has started the two of us on some strenuous exercise."

"I can see that. I am happy she is doing well. Do you have a moment to talk? It's rather important." Alveen walked to the counter, resting her forearms on the woodgrain.

"For you, Your Majesty, always." He walked around the counter and led Alveen to two chairs near the small hearth at the back of the building.

"I have a request for you, a rather large one. With King Luka and I to be married, we are going to be placing an advisor's court in charge upon my absence. We will be doing a lot of traveling back and forth. I wish for you to take a seat on that court." Masgo's expression was much like Elias's.

"Me? I am just a simple butcher, Your Majesty. I do not need higher position than where I am at."

"Are you sure? I feel you would bring a grand amount of wisdom that I don't have from being a business owner here in Cosaint for so long. I want there to be a voice of the people on my court." Masgo stared at the fire, in thought. He would look between her and his hands, tossing the idea around in his head.

"I appreciate the offer, more than you know. I understand it is a great honor, however I do wish to stay where I am at. I will be of assistance if it is needed but, I wish to spend my spare time with my family." He reached out and held her hand with a grateful smile on his face.

"Of course, I understand entirely. I appreciate your honesty, Masgo. You've always been trustworthy for that reason." She smiled and spoke with him a little longer about his family and how the business had been faring with all the attacks that had happened. She realized she had a meeting to get back to and left the butcher with no hard feelings upon his rejection. They would just have to find others that would fill the seats.

Upon entering the palace, Willow and Viktor were walking in the same direction toward the study for the meeting. They were adorable together.

"We just spoke with Sir Caspian." Willow began. "He is wonderful. A little stoic but I defiantly can tell where his loyalty lies." She was holding Viktor's arm, looking up to him as she spoke.

"That's certain. You're lucky to have such a faithful subject, as head of your guard even. He respects you greatly, Your Majesty." Viktor continued.

"That I am very much aware of. He is honest, and loyal and gives sound advice. I believe his years alongside the crown have given him much wisdom. Not to mention it would be a wonderful idea to have someone who knows battle strategy and protection of the kingdom at the head of the court." They turned to walk down the corridor toward the study. Luka and Karolyn waited outside. "I do appreciate you telling me your opinions." Alveen said genuinely as she pulled out the keys to unlock the door.

As everyone took their seats, Lovisa stood and replaced the shield, keeping their meeting private from any magical eavesdropping. Viktor began the meeting.

"I believe all of us have spoken with Sir Caspian, are we unanimous that he will be a good fit for the head of the court?" He asked around, everyone nodded in approval. "Very well. The first seat is filled. Alveen, what of the others?"

"Elias is very eager to be in such a position. He feels greatly honored to be considered. Masgo rejected his seat though." She explained plainly.

"Rejected? Why would he do that?" Viktor asked.

"He has other priorities, like his family and business. He offered to assist if a need ever arises, but he does not want to commit to a seat." Viktor rolled his eyes, not understanding the position Masgo was in.

"Very well, we will all speak with Elias, and we will continue the search for more advisors." He continued. "What of the ordeal with Tanilly? Has blood work taken place?"

"Yes. First, I would like to start off with an adoption request, from myself and King Luka for her. She is the only family I have and only heir to my line." Alveen spoke, they all waited for her to finish, "But, we have some rather unsettling news. It turns out, Tanilly is an entirely new species. She is unlike any creature on Beannithe. None of her DNA markers related to any of the creatures here. No elf or fairy in her. However, she seems to be a species with abilities far above even ours. Superior to pure blood elves, you might say." Alveen explained, waiting for reactions from her other royals.

"A new species? How is that possible?" Lovisa asked.

"I'm not sure. Unless Beannithe sensed the issue we discussed and decided to try to give us an answer." Willow suggested, running her hand over her stomach. Alveen looked at her, studying her. Something was different.

"Are you okay? You seem odd." Alveen asked her friend. Willow looked at Viktor who nodded. She smiled as she stood and addressed the table.

"There is something different. Viktor and I are expecting. Triplets." She explained. Alveen felt over joyed and envious at the same time. As much as it hurt that her friend was able to experience this joy and she would never be able to, she was also so genuinely happy for her friend.

"Oh my! Congratulations! I am so excited!" Alveen began. Everyone followed suit, asked questions and congratulating her.

"I wonder if it's a generational thing, or if it was just her." Willow expressed.

"We'll find out soon enough." Lovisa said with a smile.

"Even so, do we keep the rule in place that an heir must be majority elven to receive rights to reign? If Tanilly is not elven, that would keep her from having rights at all, leaving Cosaint and Bulgrakta without an heir. And *if* by chance, this is a generational phenomenon and Willow and Viktor's children come out as a superior species, they won't have rights either." She began to explain.

"Maybe we should not have a species restriction at all. Maybe whoever the children are, adopted or biological, have full rights." Luka interjected at something that he saw was becoming much more complicated than it needed to be.

"That's good. I would agree with that. That way if a couple is unable to conceive for any reason, there is still an opportunity for an heir. And if any of our children marry into a separate species, there is no blood work needed." Lovisa supported. The others looked around at each other. This would solve many problems. Luka and Alveen could have a rightful heir by adopting and Karolyn could adopt as well since she has never had children, giving Loxley an heir.

"I agree with that proposal. It would be beneficial to all of us." Karolyn commented.

"Then it seems to are all in agreement?" Viktor asked, looking around the table. "Very well. A new law is passed, as of today, that heirs to the thrones will be any offspring of the pure blood line, adopted or conceived. We can get into the details later, but this will be the law for now." Viktor signed the bottom of the parchment he had been writing on and passed it around, allowing everyone to read and sign it as well.

"That was eventful. Now, have we covered all issues or topics that anyone has wished to discuss?" Looking around the table, it looked like everything had been settled. "Then I close this meeting and put into place this new law that will keep the monarchy going for centuries, and put into pending the adoption for King Luka and Queen Alveen." Everyone stood as Lovisa lowered the concealment spell.

"I'd like to go tell Caspian the news." Alveen said, as the first to head toward the door.

"Let me come with you." Lovisa requested, following along. They all filed out of the room, with Alveen locking the door behind them all. They would go speak with Elias and determine his loyalty and ability to make decisions. Alveen's gown trailed behind her and she made haste toward the library where Caspian would be.

• • •

The noble centaur stood looking out the window, admiring the kingdom he protected. His white hair was glossy in the sunlight. With the sound of the new arrivals in the library, his attention was turned toward them.

"Your Majesties." He bowed with a fist over his heart. "To what do I owe the pleasure?" He asked kindly. Alveen had a large smile on her face, unable to hide how happy she was that Caspian had managed to please all the royals. He truly was one of the only citizens she fully trusted with her life.

"Our royal meeting has concluded and we have come to the unanimous agreement that, if you accept, you should be the head of the advisors court being put into place here in Cosaint. This means you will oversee all the meetings and handle business and daily routines in the absence of your Queen. Are you prepared to accept this duty?" Queen Lovisa laid out his responsibilities before him, making certain he understood what was expected of him. The centaur's chest puffed with pride as he stood tall facing the Queens. A small grin managed to grace his face.

"I would be honored, Your Majesties." He stood at attention in from of them both, glowing with confidence. Though he was sure in his abilities, that didn't mean others would believe the same. The fact that he had managed to show who he was and what he was capable of to all the royal members in the realm was a great feat for him.

"With this responsibility we also bestow upon you a gift." Lovisa continued. Alveen gave her a look of confusion

● ● ●

but followed along. She hadn't heard of any gifts for this position. "Hold out your hands please." He did as instructed and Lovisa set her hands on top of his, taking a deep breath in. You could see the dim blue light of the magic flowing through her arms and onto his hands. Pulling them away, she clasped them together behind her back. "Now think of Queen Alveen and wave your hand in front of your body like such." She demonstrated the motion for him and watched him mimic it flawlessly. A cloud of fog appeared before him, and one before Alveen. She reached out and accepted the connection of a summon. He gasped. He had just done magic. "You are now able to connect with your Queen, as it is of the utmost importance that in your role, you are loyal to her and your kingdom and what is best for both of them." He looked down at his hands, his grateful heart shining through his eyes.

"Thank-you Queen Lovisa. I don't know what else I can say." Alveen couldn't keep the smile off her face.

"I had no idea we could do that." Alveen commented to Lovisa.

"It is similar to the trials. Beannithe grants the ability, but the world has the ability to reject the applicant. It is one of the ways we confirm if we have made the right decision. It seems this time, Beannithe is in line with us. All creatures have some magic in them, most are unable to access it. All we do is pull a little of it to the surface, if it is not rejected." She explained in detail. Caspian was listening to the conversation and he could not help but be humbled as he realized the magic of their world just accepted him. *Him*, a centaur born of hardly anything that had worked hard his entire life. He bowed again to them, as they did in return, walking out of the library.

"Now" Lovisa began as they exited the library and walked slowly down the corridor. The sun shined brightly through the transparent areas of the ceiling, allowing the beams of warm light to illuminate the hallways. "It's time for wedding planning, my dear. We have a short period of time to plan this. Have you any ideas for themes and colors?" She asked trying to help her get started.

"I guess I assumed since it was a royal wedding that most of this would be chosen for me and I wouldn't get much of a say." Alveen admitted. As much as she had dreamed of planning her own wedding, she understood the importance of elegance and professionalism at a royal event.

"Why would you think that? If anything, it is meant to be a reflection of you and Luka. Let your citizens see who you are and what you believe reflects you."

"In that case, I do have quite a few ideas I would like to incorporate. How different are weddings here though? Do you have a wedding party?"

"A wedding party?" She answered confused.

"Yes, like bridesmaids and groomsmen. People that stand by you at the ceremony and get ready with you." Alveen tried explaining.

"Not really. But this is your wedding. If you want to pull from traditions back on your other world, you are able to do that. I believe it would make your wedding unique and show a part of who you are since that is where you grew up." They had reached the dining hall. Staff was moving around quickly and Willow was sitting at the table already. Alveen pointed with a confused expression

"We need to get food decision out of the way."

"Oh, Luka should really be here for this. He is very good at this sort of thing." Lovisa swiped her hand in the air before her, summoning the groom-to-be.

"Lovisa." Luka said with an annoyed tone. It looked like he was sitting in his guest chamber by the window. The sun warming his face and brightening his golden eyes.

"We need you in the dining hall. We need to make decisions on food for the wedding. Your future wife seems to think you need to be apart of it." Luka's expression lifted.

"And this is why I'm marrying her. I'll be there in a moment." He ended the connection as he stood and walked out of his room. Lovisa looked at Alveen.

"I will never understand how you managed to connect with him. The difference in him with just you being around is remarkable. He might not like most of us still but at least he's more present now." She led Alveen into the dining hall, glancing over the food placed out on the table.

"It's a mystery, I suppose." She answered. "So, we just eat all of this and decide what we like best?"

"This is the only party of wedding planning I'm sad I missed out on." Willow said as they approached her. She had already begun trying some of the appetizers that were laid out while meals were made. "I would like to request these" she pointed to two different plates, "be served before the meal. And lots of fruit. Speaking of which, can I get some fruit around here?" she asked turning her head to look for a staff member. One of the ladies nodded and headed straight to the kitchen, bringing out a large fruit tray and setting it near the Foresi Queen.

"I'm very happy you are able to help me then." Alveen laughed. Luka joined shortly after.

"This is the one part of wedding planning I do not mind being involved in." He said, rubbing his hands together as he looked over the table. He had changed out of his more formal apparel and now wore rugged jeans and a long sleeve black shirt.

"You look good." Alveen said as he sat next to her. He looked himself over and raised his eyebrow.

"Really? You like this?" he asked, unconvinced.

After trying all the trays set in front of them they moved onto the meals, which the kitchen staff brought out four small plates for them to try. Meats were prepared all different ways and the side dishes were unbelievable to Alveen's taste buds, but Luka was harder to impress. He had turned down nearly all of them, creating his own dish of pieces from each plate. When the staff brought out the combination he had requested, Alveen was proven right when she had said he would be very good at this. Desserts were easier to choose from since here they did not do a large cake, but many smaller choices.

"Alright, well now that that's decided, I'm going to leave before you begin talking of dresses and decorations." Luka stood, leaning down to give Alveen a quick kiss. "I love you. Good luck." Alveen couldn't wipe the smile off her face.

"Wait, Luka." Lovisa called after him. He stopped and slowly turned as if he had not escaped fast enough. "We do need to discuss the very real possibility of the Dorcha attacking. We must all be prepared and on alert. Especially with Samual being back."

"What is there to discuss? We agreed we moved up the wedding to try to prevent that. We want to enjoy this day also. We will all be aware of the possibility and take the proper precautions. I don't want fear hanging over us on a day like this. We have nothing to be afraid of." He said as he walked quickly out of the dining hall.

"I guess we will just make sure we have any weapons on our bodies and strategically place them as needed. We'll get to that part later though." Alveen continued the topic. "Now, seriously, this is what I'm thinking as far as my dress, the decorations and some smaller details." She continued on with Lovisa and Willow intently listening, objecting or approving of her ideas. Alveen had done plenty of thinking and had much of it planned out already. All that was needed was a custom gown, and Lovisa had offered to handle the rest.

Alveen waited in the Queen's chamber for Mysti since she was in charge of the gown. Karolyn had joined them now. She sat in a chair, looking over all the notes for the wedding, nodding or raising an eyebrow at things she found curious.

"Ah, Your Majesty. I am honored that you have chosen me to design your gown. I wasn't sure if you were serious." Mysti said as she entered the room behind Lovisa.

"I believe in your abilities. You have created multiple other gowns I love." Alveen said, thinking of how much detail her dress would require.

"Of course. Now tell me about this gown. What styles are we thinking, materials, accents and such. Paint me a picture, Your Majesty."

~Chapter VIII~
The Royal Wedding

Citizens woke that day, excited for a new beginning in their kingdom. Not only was it still early in their new Queen's reign, but she was creating an alliance with a kingdom that had long been separated from the rest.

Alveen prepared in the Queen's chamber listening to the three Princesses laughing as they ran around with fancy hair and dresses. Each of them wore a black organza gown. Gold glitter peeked out from underneath the sheer fabric on their skirts. The bodices were black satin with cap sleeves, wrapped in elegantly folded golden glitter tulle. Alveen winced as Mysti pulled on her hair to twist it into the chosen style.

"I am so excited for you. Are you nervous at all?" Queen Lovisa asked as she twisted her fingers, making sure her hair was curled properly and hanging where it needed to be. All the Queen's and Mysti wore different colored dark gowns. Each the closest to their own countries color. Lovisa wore a navy one-shouldered gown, created from a jersey material with tulle of the exact color lying flat over it. Willow had grown quite a bit even in the mere two weeks since Alveen had seen her last, which they expected when planning gowns. Her hunter green gown was of the same materials as the others but her waist line sat higher at an empire, in order to give room for her pregnant stomach that was now all too obvious. Her one shoulder had a tulle watteau train trailing behind her. She had straightened her short brown hair and pinned back a braid to keep her hair looking formal. Karolyn wore the color of Cosaint, a burgundy one shouldered gown matching the others. Her hair was a mimic for Willow's since it too was short.

"I'm not nervous at all actually. I just feel like it is about time I am able to marry the love of my life. I might have gone crazy if I waited longer." She admitted. Mysti still pulled on her hair, but Alveen could see her in the vanity mirror. She wore a gown much like Karolyn's only she had an overlay of gold glitter tulle like the younger girl, but matched the others with one shoulder and a tulle train from the shoulder. She stood out because she would be her maid of honor. Mysti had been by her side through so much and had taken care of Tanilly when she needed someone. Mysti had spun her around multiple times as she would change the way she did her hair.

"Are you ready to see?" Mysti asked excited, clapping her hands. She spun Alveen around. The other gathered around the mirror to look at the Queen with her makeup and hair done perfectly for her day. Short curls hung loose by her face in front of a set of three braids, one small, one large and one a little bit looser in design that wrapped around her head, encapsulating a large bun of loose, glossy curls, high enough for her to place her custom designed crown around it and not interfere with the structure of the masterpiece Mysti created.

"Oh I love it. It is exactly like what I was describing." Mysti reached into a black satin lined box, pulling out a crown Alveen had designed herself. A large circular tiara was placed in front of her, with peaks the height of her hair and valleys that hid within the hair on her head for they were so thin. You could hardly see the metal on the crown for it was covered entirely of crystals, sparkly with every small movement of her head. Her makeup was done more natural, but her eyes were dramatic and dark. The black shadow faded into the golden glitter on her lids, and her eye lashes had doubled in length, creating a focus on her eyes.

"Oh Alveen!" Lovisa reached for her hand. "You look so beautiful." She pushed a curl out of Alveen's face and continued, "Let's see the dress!!" Lovisa exclaimed standing back by the other Queen's. Alveen stepped lightly across the stone under her feet as she entered the bathroom. Her gown hung up on the far wall, out of site to everyone except herself and Mysti. Slipping into the gown, she admired herself in the wall sized mirror. Unlike the traditional wedding gowns she had been used to, she chose to shine in a glittering light gold hue. It consisted of two layers, the first being a sheath gown with high slits revealing both legs. Covered in detailed applique, it cinched at her hips and flowed loosely down her legs. Her back was covered in sporadic applique to give the illusion of the gown dissolving up her back. A sheer layer covered her shoulders and connected the applique along her bare back to the sweetheart neckline that had been encrusted with heavily glittered applique. Her sleeves were sheer as well, the only applique and lace added were fitted to her forearms and wrapped around her upper arms to make it look as if she wore off the shoulder sleeves. So much detail and thought had been put into this one dress. A second ballgown layer was attached at her hips, detachable if necessary. One of the biggest requests Alveen had for Mysti while designing was for her to be able to fight at a moment notice if the need came. The detachable layer was a shimmering taffeta with a few layers of golden glitter tulle covered by organza to keep the glitter in place.

"Alveen!" Lovisa gasped her name in awe of the piece of clothing. "This gown lives up to this momentous occasion." Lovisa said as Alveen stepped out and spun to reveal the detailed back as well. Willow and Karolyn admired the gown as well.

"This certainly fits you, Your Majesty." Willow said with a smile. "So much detail and functional as well." She said noting the slits when Alveen detached the skirt to show them the sheath gown.

"He's going to be blinded by your beauty." Karolyn commented on how much sparkle and character the gown had. She was more of a simple appearance woman, which was not at all bad, but that was not how Alveen was.

Standing in Alveen's old room, Luka looked out the window at the front lawn being set up and designed as his bride-to-be had desired. Cosaint glittered on every corner. The staff and volunteers had spoken with Queen Alveen and came up with a design she would never forget. On the lawn between the palace and the bay is where they decided to exchange their promises. Those with the ability to manipulate nature flew along the branches that hung out over the lawn, covering them in a hanging moss sprinkled with glitter, giving them the most whimsical effect. A few reached into the soil, calling on more trees to grow in order to support the design they created. In a large circle, new trees grew tall, their branches hanging and intertwining with one another just as the creatures had commanded in order to hang the chandelier that would hang over the heads of the newly-wed couple. He had to admit, as much as he wanted to disagree and have his own twist on the event, she had done an amazing job and put so much thought into it. With their engagement party representing the ice kingdom that he was known for, the wedding represented her as much as the enchanted forest she reigned over.

Alveen had trusted his judgement on his outfit for the occasion, seeing as he had always impressed her with how well put together he was. As usual, black was his go-to. His suit was matte black with satin black lapel and underneath his suit jacket was a black button up and a satin black tie. He also refused to wear dress shoes, so they had agreed upon a black matte pair of dress boots they had found.

"You don't think that's too much black?" Viktor asked him, looking his friend over as the time became close for them to head down to the ceremony. Luka did not respond to such a foolish comment.

"Well, their main colors are black and gold, King Viktor. I think it is a very unique, statement outfit. Which is fitting for this event." Caspian chimed in. Luka had only allowed the two of them and a couple of his guards to be in the room, not that he needed them there. They decided to have a small wedding party, but they would not walk down the aisle, they would simply sit in the front row as a show of support and approval. Viktor wore a navy suit jacket with his black pants and dress shoes, his hair combed and tied back at his neck. Caspian looked out the window at the sun. "Alright, Your Majesties, it is time to take your places for the ceremony." Luka nodded and walked out the chamber door, fixing his shirt cuffs, followed by his entourage of guards.

Moss hung from trees, and glittered as the falling sun's rays reflected off of them. Candles were placed sporadically around in spheres as to not allow the flames to touch the recently grown trees that now formed the events location. The glow from the flames wrapped around the tree trucks and through all the branches and hanging moss. Centerpieces involved more candles and wreaths of branches, leaves and darkly hued floral. As the sun began to fall from the sky, the golden glow cued the beginning of a historical wedding.

"Don't be nervous." Viktor said as he passed Luka to take his seat. Nervous? What would he have to be nervous about. If anything, he was alert and ready for an attack at any moment. Both of his calves were wrapped with holsters for his daggers and underneath his black suit jacket were more weapons should he need them. He refused to be caught off guard.

A melodic song began to play on a distant piano with string instruments joining in for a beautiful instrumental song. Luka took a deep breath as he was snapped back into the present moment. He was getting married and his wife-to-be would have no problem expressing her dissatisfaction if he were distracted and emotionless on such an important day.

Stepping out from beside the ramp of the palace entry, he made his way down the lawn where a glorious archway of vines and lights awaited for him to pass through. Unlike other events, citizens were smiling as he walked past, kicking up flower petals that were scattered across the aisle. He observed the chandeliers above the walkway and the flicker of the flames, trying not to focus on those around him.

Caspian stood at the center of the opening that the aisle led to. A large tree behind him had thick branches twisted and tangled to form the layout Alveen had wanted. The branches created archways and chandeliers from which staff members had manipulated many species of moss to hang perfectly from. They hung gemstones and crystals strategically so they would reflect the sunset. The design truly was perfect in the representation of them as a couple. Black represented Luka and his silence, the fear that followed him and the iron from which his kingdom was created, but there was no better color to represent her than gold. Though they were the colors of his kingdom, nothing shined quite like she did in the color of the Solas kingdoms. She was the light he was meant to find after he had been walked down a tunnel of darkness for so long. As true as it all was, he came to another realization. He could be standing in the middle of a muddy field and she could approach him wearing ripped and tattered clothing and he wouldn't feel any less emotional about this moment. He just wanted to see his love, the one that changed his entire outlook on being a King.

After what seemed like long minutes, she emerged, walking down the lawn in the same path he had. Her gown sparkled more than the decorations around her. Even in her glorious regal ensemble she wore now, with her make-up and hair done to perfection, all he could focus on were her eyes of teal and gold, and her smile. She was smiling at him.

She looked at Luka, standing in the sporadic pile of flower petals with the warm and cozy glow of the candles and the sunset around them, in his suit of entirely black, and she couldn't help but relax, knowing she was making the best decision ever. The man who worked for her affection and didn't give up when their kingdoms experienced hardship, was waiting to marry her. Her, the girl who was still new to so many concepts this world held and was possibly the most stubborn creature there was.

As their eyes met all Luka could think was how lucky he was that she chose him. She was his. He didn't know what he had done to deserve someone so genuine and stubborn and different than the rest. He had always imagined he would marry out of obligation, never, not once in his mind, did he think he would find someone that made him question everything and never want to look back, but there she was. Whether dressed in glittering gold, like the calm sunrise after a snow and ice storm as she was now, or covered in dirt and sweat coming from battle or a hunt, she mesmerized him.

"You clean up well." She whispered to him as she stepped beside him.

"I doubt anyone notices me right now. You are..." he couldn't find the word to describe how powerful she made him feel just by standing beside him.

"Thank-you." She said, not needing him to find that word. As they stood there, ready to make a promise to each other, him in all black and her in sparkling gold and white, no two people ever looked more different. No two people ever were more different than the two of them, yet somehow, it worked.

The ceremony was short and emotional, with the citizens watching as they promised to reign in unison and protect each other. The sun was now behind the mountains, leaving a magical glow in the sky, but leaving the lawn to be only lit by the lights and flickering candles. The area now looked romantic and warm, though a cold breeze still blew past. Below the expansive chandelier of antlers, moss, crystals and lights, they made the promises that would be written in history books. With two cords, their wrists were tied together to represent their kingdoms and their devotion now to the other kingdoms.

"Stand for Their Majesties of Cosaint and Bulgrakta, husband and wife, King Luka and Queen Alveen." Caspian declared as Alveen and Luka shared a kiss, unable to keep from smiling. Their hands were untied and they walked around the oversized tree to the dance floor, where all of the couples would dance to an instrumental song they had chosen, their first dance as a married couple. Pan flutes, pianos and string instruments harmoniously blended to form the melody.

Many loved ones joined hands, twirling and holding each other close in a warm light of the flames and lights. Alveen and Luka didn't have to say a thing, they knew just by looking in each other's eyes how happy and grateful the other was. Leaves began to fall from the trees, making the evening more romantic. Alveen looked up into the tree to admire the lights and flowers. Her heart caught in her chest when she realized why the leaves had fallen.

"They're here." Alveen quickly whispered to Luka, pushing him away from her. She twirled to the side of the dance floor, detaching her ballgown skirt to reveal her legs peeking through the slits, lined with holsters. A figure fell from the tree just above where they had been standing. Luka stood with his daggers in hand, Alveen resorted to her magic first, harnessing it in her palms.

The hood flipped back to reveal the clean-shaven face of Samual. He looked like he had before, only with barren eyes. His soul had moved on, leaving his body empty and ready to carry out orders plunged into him.

"And here I thought we would be the ones getting married." He jested towards Alveen, looking her up and down in her wedding gown. Luka's face had begun to turn red. Alveen didn't have time for this. She hurled the electrical orbs of magic at him, surely enough to obliterated him. With speedy reflexes as he had before, he managed to escape her weapons, only to clash with Luka who managed to be quite graceful despite his size. Alveen ran up, her arms tingling with magic crying to be released. With enough momentum she thrust her arm forward, releasing a wave of quick moving fog to surround Samual. While he was in the fog it would make him confused and unable to focus. Luka stepped back, protectively guarding Alveen. Samual laughed from inside the fog. He was stumbling around. Lovisa stepped up to Alveen's side, ready to help defend those around them. Alveen released the fog, preparing to jump into the fight should Luka and Lovisa need assistance.

The guards were leading the citizens away from the event. Zakarian's minions began to pour into the area, though they were hardly a match for the guards on duty today.

With a shake of his head, Samual lunged at Luka, hoping to push him aside and get directly to Alveen. Luka was thrust aside by an unseen force, only for his body to be replaced by Lovisa's. Luka's heart stopped for a moment and Alveen's stomach turned as they saw Samual drive his sword through Lovisa's chest. Silence followed as Samual stood there, smiling down on the bleeding Queen. His gaze quickly snapped to Alveen, not forgetting his purpose for coming here; to kill the all-powerful elven monarch of Cosaint.

"Get Lovisa to the healer's quarters. They may be able to save her yet. Her elven blood makes her resilient." Luka ordered guards that had come over to aid. The blow wouldn't kill her. Elven blood had magic running through it, speeding any healing process.

Without notice, Caspian bounded over them and towards Samual who was still heading directly towards Alveen. She braced herself and summoned the magic again, this time pulling from the flames around them. As she began walking towards him, Caspian drove his oversized sword between his shoulder blade, severing his spine as the sword revealed itself from his chest. Samual froze, but began to laugh. It was as if his body felt no pain, he was simply a hollow vessel for the demonic spirit that had been placed inside him. Alveen swung her arms around forcing the flames to grow and travel towards her foe. Heat licked his legs as he was quickly swallowed up, laughing as he turned to ashes yet again. Alveen's heart was in her stomach. Though she knew that was not really Samual, it was like a nightmare brought to life as she caused his demise.

"We should bury or contain his ashes to ensure they can not repeat the awakening of his body." Viktor spoke. He had been defending his pregnant Queen on the other side of the lawn.

"I cannot believe you wouldn't let me fight. Being pregnant does not make me incapable of doing everything." Willow spat at him, frustrated that she had to be a damsel in distress. That was certainly not going to be okay with her.

"My dear, I only wish for you to be safe. You are proud and I know you will not tell me if you feel incapable." Viktor responded with a smile.

"I will tell you if I feel something is wrong. Right now, I am perfectly capable of fighting and defending myself and others." She glared at him but gave him a quick kiss as she walked away. "I'm going to see to Lovisa."

"We should go as well." Alveen suggested. Luka had slowly made his way to her side with an unreadable expression. "Hey." Alveen thrust her open palm into his chest, stopping him in his tracks as she planted herself in front of him. "You had no idea what she was going to do. You were trying to defend us, just as she was." Alveen could see a sliver of guilt in his expression. He nodded in understanding.

"I don't feel guilty at all. I'm not the one who did this to her." He said quietly, composed.

"No. You're not." She stared for a second, she could tell that he wasn't sure if he believed the words he spoke. "You're also not a very good liar." She walked away with Viktor and Willow, Luka trailing them. She was not going to stand and argue with him about his emotions.

Walking across the village you would have never known there was an attack. The intruders with Samual must have been minimal since the damage didn't extend beyond the borders of the event and the music still played lively throughout the streets. Many must not even have known what happened, she guessed, watching them stumble around with drunken smiles and laughs.

"Up those stairs. We had to re-locate the healers." Alveen explained. The earthquake before had destroyed the buildings all around the training ground, including the healing chambers that were once there. Alveen stepped forward and led her peers through the moss-covered twisted branches that formed the doorway. Logs had been flattened and molded from the many people that had walked up and down the staircase they now ascended. The side walls were covered in bioluminescent vines that emitted a white glow, allowing them to see their path.

Reaching the top of the staircase, multiple witches, warlocks and healers were frantically running around. The

Royals all exchanged glances. "Excuse me. Where is Queen Lovisa?" Willow yelled out. A short man gestured them to follow him. A few citizens had been injured. Thankfully, none of them looked to be too serious.

"Please wait here." The young warlock stopped them at the doorway. The room ahead was filled with quick working healers. Them being in the room would only have gotten in the way. "We are doing what we can but we fear there may have been a poison of sorts on the blade." With that, he walked in, leaving them to wonder.

"Do you think it's the same poison?" Viktor asked? "The same one they used on Hunter and Vailion?" He asked the group around him.

"I don't know. I think that would be too quick of a sacrifice for that to work the way they need it to. Plus, the portal is closed. What good would her sacrifice bring them this time?" Willow explained with her brows pinched together in thought.

The newly wed Queen of Cosaint paced back and forth in the doorway, her husband watching her intently. Luka reached out his hand without saying a word, only looking at his beautiful wife, still in her gown, which he was amazed was unaffected and undamaged. He didn't feel guilt for what happened to Lovisa, he knew that he personally had done nothing wrong that caused her current condition. Alveen always tried so hard, though, to make sure he was okay and make certain that he was tended to and well. Something no one in the world had ever done for him on such a level. Though their wedding day was interrupted and had led to injuries, in this moment, all he could think was how lucky he was that he was officially married to Queen Alveen. She looked at his hand and then to his eyes, wondering what was going through his head. As she intertwined her fingers with his, he pulled her close to just hold her.

"Are you okay?" She asked quietly. He looked in her eyes, admiring the uniqueness they shined.

"I truly am." She leaned against his chest, impatiently waiting for the healers diagnosis of Lovisa. Willow and Viktor had decided to leave, waiting for word instead of standing and waiting. Luka and Alveen sat on a bench outside the room, unable to see inside.

"Your Majesties?" The young man came back out of the room. Alveen jumped up, ready to hear an update. She turned and looked past him into the room. The bed was empty. Her heart jumped and her shoulders relaxed.

"Is she up already? Or was she moved to recovery?" Alveen asked confidently. The young warlock looked between Luka and Alveen, his eyes pouring over with sorrow.

"Your Majesty, we did everything within our powers. Whatever was on that blade prevented her from healing. It was as if it blocked her magic, not allowing her body to access it." He looked at his Queen. She was only slowly beginning to understand. "She's gone." He finally said the words. The only words that would leave her speechless and heartbroken.

"Thank-you for everything you've done. Please ensure her body is prepared to be transported back to Irielle." Luka said quickly, holding onto Alveen and leading her down the stairs, back to the palace. She was in shock, not fully aware of what was going on around her as they walked. Luka ensured to have a steady grip on her to lead her home.

"How am I going to tell them?" She whispered as they walked alone down the cobblestone street. The village had gone silent for the most part at this early hour of the morning. Alveen and Luka hadn't slept yet.

"I'll tell Viktor, Willow and Karolyn. Viktor is my cousin after all." He said reassuring her that there was no need to worry. She finally snapped her head towards him, tears trailing down her face that was still composed, unrevealing to the emotions she felt otherwise.

"No, I mean the twins." She said bluntly. Luka's eyes widened slightly. He hadn't even thought about her daughters. "Her only children. Young girls still. How am I supposed to look two little girls in the eye and tell them?" He walked quietly, thinking.

"We will do it together. We will both be there for them."

"And where does this leave Irielle? They have no other leader. Both of their future monarchs are only children, unmarked by the trials still." She began to get herself worked up as she thought of all this meant. Luka stepped quickly in front of her, holding her shoulders so she looked him in the eyes.

"Alveen. Calm. Down." He spoke slowly, emphasizing each word quietly to her. "As terrible as it is to lose anyone, there are rules and procedures in place for when something of this magnitude happens. The other monarchs will rule over together. We will have another meeting to decide how we will be present in the kingdom, until such a time as a new monarch is ready to take the throne again." She took a deep breath as she heard his words. His voice. Oh, his voice made her so calm and relaxed. She wrapped her arms around his waist and walked with him into the palace, up the ramp and through the doorless entryway.

The Royals of Foresi, Krumvite and Loxley were summoned to the throne room. As they all entered with a thousand questions in their eyes, Luka took a small breath in as he stepped forward. Alveen stood by his side, her emotion showing through her rosey red cheeks. She stood tall. There was never going to be a time she was emotionally immune to everyone she loved dying as casualties to this on-going, childish war.

"The Queen is dead. The weapon used on her had been dipped in a poison that blocked her magic from healing." Luka was blunt and to the point because that was exactly what they needed to hear. They didn't want someone circling around the question or trying to sugar coat the reality of their situation.

● ● ●

Willow's face became pinched as she held her emotions back. She took a deep breath in, allowing only a single tear to escape. Karolyn rested her head in her hands, trying to comprehend that yet another of their monarch had fallen. Karolyn was the last of her generation.

"Thank-you for informing us." Viktor replied. "Those poor girls."

"We are off to speak with them now. I believe a meeting should be conducted as we now have a kingdom without a leader. Decisions must be made." Alveen spoke confidently, putting her emotions on hold for a moment. Gracefully, her and her new husband exited the throne room, making their way towards the Queen's chambers where the girls were instructed to be taken during the attack.

Alveen had been a pace or two ahead of Luka. He sped up enough to reach out and grasp her hand, pulling her to a halt in the corridor. He looked at her with concern. He could see her eyes reflecting the lights around them as they glistened over with angry tears she was desperately trying to hold back. If there was one thing he knew with certainty about his wife, it was that her soul was one of fire. Her passion, her energy, her anger... she was fierce and her emotions would take over if she didn't allow them out.

"It's okay." He said, not needing her to say anything. He pulled her towards his chest, allowing her a moment to break down midst the thousands of moments she had to hold herself together. Luka had been trained how to handle deaths

● ● ●

and how to control and handle his emotions. Alveen had never gone through that, but that was something he loved about her. She was raw and so full of her emotions that it always gave him reassurance in the good and the humanity of the world that wasn't even a home to humans.

"I am so sick of this war. I am done with everyone dying for no particular cause other than hate and selfishness, and I am through with being the kind of Queen that allows this." She was still leaning against him as she spoke her feelings of being frustrated. "Why me? Why did I have to be the one born into all of this only for all the goodness to be ripped away?" She rested her head on his chest, feeling his arms hold her tighter. "I cannot lose you and Tanilly." She finally admitted her fear. Her fear of being alone and losing everyone around her.

"Look at me." He stepped back, still holding her, and looked her in the eyes. "You were born into this because no one else could handle the pressure. No one else would be able to take on the emotional strife you have. You are meant to restore the balance of this world. You are meant to once and for all end the era of the Dorcha."

"You do all of this without even blinking or asking anyone for help. I come to you so often. What kind of Queen does that make me?" She brought her hands to her face, ashamed.

"That makes you wise and brave. No one was meant to do this alone, that is why the monarchy was created. I don't normally have a reason to ask for aide, remember I'm not the one that has been a target since birth." He explained. "Let go get this over with so we can get the meeting started." He searched her eyes and placed a small kiss on her forehead, reaching down to hold her hand and talk to the girls together.

The guards outside the chamber door opened it for them, revealing the three girls on Alveen's bed with sorrowful looks. Alveen and Luka exchanged glances. How could they know already?

"Girls, we've come to talk to you." Luka spoke softly. Tanilly turned towards them, her eyes glowing a bright pink.

"They know already." She said simply. "I told them. But they understand." Alveen and Luka were confused to say the least.

"Tanilly, how did you know what happened?" Alveen asked, gesturing for her to come towards her so the conversation was a little more private. She looked down at her feet as she spoke to her aunt.

"I overheard. In my head. I was sitting in here and all of a sudden your thoughts poured into my mind. I could hear everything. I knew you were worried to tell them, so I did. And I helped them understand that it was to defend you and Luka and that she will never be forgotten." Her sweet innocent voice explained.

"Wait.." Luka looked between them, "Did you say you hear her thoughts?" His eyes were wide as he tried to comprehend the magic at play. It seemed Tanilly's power was stronger than they knew.

"Yes, we discovered we have a mutual ability, but before it was only when we touched. Apparently it has gotten stronger." Alveen reached out to Tanilly, holding her hands to let her know she was not mad at her for what she had done. As Tanilly's hands rested in hers, a calmness washed over her, followed by confidence. Her insecurities that she had just spoken of, vanished from her heart and were replaced by iron walls of strength. Alveen pulled her hands away slowly so she didn't startle Tanilly. "How did you do that?" Alveen asked quietly. She looked to the little girls. "This is why they're so calm, isn't it?" Tanilly nodded, still looking at her feet.

"I only just found out I could do it. I thought it would be a way to use it for good." She explained.

"What happened?" Luka asked, still shocked on the sidelines.

"She has empathetic powers also. She can control emotions." Alveen stood up, stunned by this discovery.

"How is that possible? That's against the guidelines, isn't it?" He asked, taking in all the new information he was receiving.

"I'm not sure. It certainly has the possibility to be, but the way she is using it is not for manipulative purposes." She looked back to the young girl. "Sweetie, you need to let them grieve. What you did was very thoughtful, but everyone must have the ability to determine how they feel." Alveen explained. "Do you understand?" Tanilly shook her head with a small smile and released the small hold she had on the twins. As the wall fell inside them, grief overflowed. Tears flowed and sorrow-filled wails echoed through the chamber. Luka and Alveen ran towards them, holding them in their arms and comforting them in their time of pain and loss. They could only stay with them for a short time. A leader of Irielle had to be decided.

They bid their farewells to the girls, allowing them to sleep in her chamber. As they walked out the door, the other royals already waited outside the conference room. Alveen unlocked the solid door allowing everyone to file in and waited for Willow to put a protection spell around the room. She nodded when it was finished.

"Alright, let's get to the point. We need to know who will take responsibility of the twins and how we will go about choosing a new leader for Irielle until the girls are able to take power." Viktor spoke bluntly to the others. He pulled out a folder from a shelf he had passed. "These are the wishes of our dear Queen Lovisa." He tossed it down on the table. "I have already looked through it. It states that Alveen is given guardianship of the two girls and we shall share power until they come of age." He explained with a less than amused smile. Alveen was surprised by the new information.

"Me? Why did she choose me? She hasn't known me long." Alveen spoke though it seemed to be more to herself then directed at one person. Alveen loved the girls, but with

Tanilly's power growing she was unsure if it was wise for them to be around. Tanilly could help train them and they could learn a lot. Were they ready to go from zero children to three? Alveen looked back and forth to Luka and the others and a thought entered her mind. "I have a counterproposal, if Queen Karolyn is in agreement." She looked at her and she gave an expression letting everyone know she was just as confused. "Luka and I have been blessed with a child already. I propose that if she wants to make the time, Queen Karolyn becomes the guardian. She is closest to the kingdom and if she raises them up to be a rightful Queen, one of them could become the heir of Loxley while the other takes power back over Irielle." She explained her genius plan. Karolyn was the last of her generation and they couldn't face this issue again. Loxley would need an heir and Karolyn would be the perfect Queen to raise them up properly and ensure they were taught all about the right ways to rule. They would learn so much through her. Everyone looked to Karolyn.

"Um.. The document states she wishes for them to be with you, Queen Alveen. Not me." Karolyn stated with a small shake in her voice.

"I understand this. However, we are in a very different situation here as we are almost entirely heirless. We have changed the law so you may have an adopted heir, and if it were Ava or Brielle then they would have access to magic and as long as they pass the trials, Loxley will go on." Alveen explained simply. Everyone looked between each other, in agreement and understanding. "If you wish that is, I mean not to force this upon you. I simply thought it would be worth discussing." Karolyn pondered her nieces thoughts for a few moments.

"I suppose that wouldn't be a bad idea to strategically place them for the good of Beannithe. But what of Irielle? I cannot run two countries and raise and train two girls." Karolyn pointed out to the royals around her.

"The guidelines state that we can all rule over Irielle in a time such as this. We take turns appearing in the kingdom, but now we are left with another duty of ensuring the safety of the advisors council that now sits in Irielle." Viktor expressed as he flipped through the book of laws and procedures that he had pulled off a dusty shelf. Willow sat in the background, aware that in the coming months she would be unable to do much traveling and couldn't exert herself and stress herself with running two kingdoms.

"We shall depart once our council is set for Cosaint. Bulgrakta will be fine with myself being absent for a while, however I will need to return and stay for an extended period of time once all of this is complete." Luka stated simply. He was very talented when it came to not allowing stressful situations to overwhelm him. "Unless my wife thinks otherwise?" he raised an eyebrow to the beautiful elf standing near him, still in her detailed and battle-ready wedding gown.

"I believe that's a fine idea. Between the two of us, and King Viktor if you choose, we can ensure that Irielle is run properly until such a time that someone can sit upon their throne. We will need to sit down with the three advisors councils and come up with an appropriate travel schedule in order to give the proper time and appearances in each kingdom." She analyzed as she spoke, explaining the few obstacles in their way, though her tone suggested they would make this plan work, even if it was inconvenient for them.

"All in agreement?" Queen Karolyn asked, searching the eyes of each of the royals. King Viktor nodded in agreement as well. "It will not be easy, but we must all come to agreement that should any problems arise or any of you are unable to continue this agreement, a meeting will be called immediately." Her tone and expressions gave away that she thought they would not be able to handle the stress of the traveling between kingdoms and constant running multiple kingdoms with different cultures. Alveen knew because that was exactly how she felt. It may work for a while but balancing her marriage and her duty as Queen was not going to be an easy feat. "Very well. Off to set in the council here and discuss the decision. Then Luka and Alveen, you will be the first to go back to Irielle with the girls and establish a trustworthy council to rule in your absence. I will send for the girls while you are there." Karolyn stood and exited the room.

Knowing what the task at hand was, the newlywed couple exited the conference room, locking the door behind. The day had been long on everyone.

"Perhaps we should retreat to my chamber and rest. We can speak with the council in the morning." Luka suggested, keeping his voice low. Alveen looked back at him, not expecting to see the smile on his face. It was their wedding night, she remembered suddenly. With everything else going on, she hardly was aware that she still wore her gown. He reached his arm around, wrapping it around her waist and pulling her in for a slow, appreciative kiss.

"That may be for the best, really." She responded, followed by a kiss on his neck and intertwining her fingers behind his head. Luka had been staying in her old chamber. As they made their way across the palace, Luka continued to pull her close. Though this would be Alveen's first time with anyone, she wasn't nervous at all. She felt comfortable and relaxed around her new husband and trusted him with her life.

As they passed through her familiar threshold, she was swept off her feet and her lips were met with a fierce and hungry kiss. Alveen was distracted from the bittersweet day that had passed and the stress of what was to come as her new husband admired her before setting her down and covering the floor in front of the fireplace with his fur cape that hung over the back of the chair. He returned to her, wrapping his muscular arms around her waist again, running his hand along her back.

"You are mesmerizing. In case I forgot to tell you that." He whispered as he kissed her again.

"You did, but I suppose I can forgive you." She smiled as she lead him towards the fire, facing him as he walked backwards. He spun her around slowly, beginning to reach for the clasps on her gown. He brought his lips to her neck, allowing a quiet, seductive growl to escape his throat as her

● ● ●

gown loosened around her. Every part of her wanted to make a sarcastic comment or joke, but she simply couldn't find the words as he lifted her into his arms.

~Chapter IX~
Irielle

Luka rolled over, kissing his wife's shoulder as they lay cuddled together with the soft fur against their skin and the warmth from the flames in the hearth filling the air around them. He could see the sun peeking through the edges of the curtains, letting him know they needed to get a start on their day. He admired Alveen for a few moments before disturbing her peaceful state.

"My Queen, it's time to wake up." He whispered close to her. She pushed herself up onto her arm quickly, being startled by his voice. He leaned back, thankful that she didn't head butt him in the face. "Well good morning, sunshine." He chuckled. She smiled and allowed herself to lay back down for a minute before making her way to the bathroom to get ready.

"Good morning to you as well my handsome King." She smiled, cuddling with a pillow and peeking at him. "I'm surprised you're awake at this hour." She was always more of a morning person than he had been.

"It seems I got a restful night sleep." He looked her over one last time, "It must have been the company." He stood up, walking to the bathroom to shower before preparing for the day.

Luka waited for Alveen in front of the fireplace as she was pulling her boots on. "I need to stop in the dungeon before we leave." She stated. Luka raised his brow, taken by surprise at this statement.

"And why is that?" he asked, confused.

"I believe Killian has more answers, or at least information he can share. I believe it would be beneficial to take him with us and learn what we can while we are away. I want to determine if he is safe though. No one has come looking for him and he has not given us any problems. I truly believe they think he is dead and that he betrayed them." Luka stared at his wife, but his thoughts were flying through his head faster than he could speak them.

"Are you sure that's the best choice? We have many responsibilities while we are away, and he may just be a distraction to you." Luka wasn't sure how he felt about her idea, but in his head he knew that she always had some of the best instincts. Alveen looked at him and smiled confidently. "Very well. I will stand by this crazy choice you are making." He rolled his eyes and let out a sigh, only to be greeted by a quick kiss.

"Thank-you." She walked out the door with him on her heels, ready to stand by and be a second opinion for the old generation's prince and his father in law.

Luka reached out and held Alveen's hand. Though he may not always agree with her madness and crazy way, he supported her and knew her intentions were always in the right place. As they descended the stairs to the level below, natural light became more scarce but white orbs illuminated the walkways and rooms from either the ceiling or walls. Guards were placed sporadically throughout the stone corridor.

"Your Majesties." One of the guards at the end of the hall addressed them. "To what do we owe the pleasure?"

"I need to speak with Killian." He stated. She knew he had been moved to a more comfortable cell, but she really had no idea what that meant for him. The guard nodded, gesturing for them to follow him down another hall with only a few doors. He approached the last door on the left, unlocking it with a small key that glowed as it was turned. Alveen nodded to him as she entered with Luka.

Alveen looked around the room. The walls were painted white, along with the floor. The room had a door that looked like it led to a bathroom and an average sized bed against the far wall. A few book shelves stood tall against the stone walls, but other then those few items, it still looked like a jail cell to her.

"Nice to see you Killian." She addressed the man sitting on the bed with a book.

"Alveen. I was wondering when I would get a chance to speak with you again." His face still looked as distraught as it had been the night he regained his memories. He attempted a weak smile. "I hear there was a royal wedding." The disowned Prince looked past Alveen to the King behind her. "Am I right to assume it was for the two of you?" he asked, his voice breaking.

"Yes. Cosaint and Bulgrakta have aligned." Alveen said, trying to sound professional and diplomatic. She still had no idea what his intentions were and giving him fuel was the last thing she wanted. "But that's not why I've come here. I believe you have answers and information that could be greatly useful to us." She spoke bluntly.

"I have told you everything I know, Alveen. I promise you. I was not part of organizing or planning or plotting as it would be." He explained, slowly standing up from his bed. His body had begun to weaken and his muscle mass and greatly decreased since the last time she saw him.

"What are your intentions here? Hypothetically, what would your agenda be if you ever leave this cell?" She asked him with a sweet voice that carried through the room. She couldn't tell but her eyes had begun to glow gold and teal. Luka began talking behind her.

• • •

"My intentions are to protect you and ensure safe decisions are made. When I leave this cell, my agenda will include making safe passage to Irielle where we will choose who sits upon the advisors council." Luka wasn't blinking. Alveen turned, confused as to why he answered, and then Killian began to talk.

"My intentions are nothing. When I leave this cell, I have no agenda. I recognize my loyalties were wrong and I only choose to right those wrongs that were done." Killian didn't blink either. Alveen stepped back, watching her husband and father stare blankly at her. What was wrong with them?

"Stop. Whatever you're doing stop." She said softly. Her voice carried again, melodically. Both of them blinked quickly, releasing a breath they had been unintentionally holding in. Luka looked around and met her gaze. He wouldn't question her now, in front of someone who was potentially untrustworthy.

"Killian, You will travel with us to Irielle. I wish to learn what you know and discover just how true your intentions are." She walked out of the room following Luka. She addressed the guard next. "He will be coming with us. Please ensure he is prepared for travel within the hour." Alveen continued walking and followed Luka up the stairs. When they entered the corridor, Luka stopped her, looking around for eavesdroppers.

"What was that? What did you do?" He questioned. He had never been afraid of her or her magic before, though he knew she was powerful and had magnificent abilities, but she was able to manipulate his actions and that was not supposed to be magically possible.

"I have no idea. I didn't even mean to do whatever it was."

"Alveen, I had no control. It was as if I was forced to tell you what you were asking. I didn't choose to reply with my intentions or answer your questions." Alveen stared at him. Nothing about his demeanor in the cell or now suggested that he was kidding or playing a trick on her. How could she compel anyone, especially without knowing?

"I swear, I didn't mean to do that to you. Why would I have used that on you at that time? That did nothing for me." Luka ran his hand through his hair. He looked frustrated and confused.

"I'm not upset with you. I just don't understand what's going on. First Tanilly has unspeakable powers, that seem to be increasing everyday and now you are also adding to your collection of abilities. It's wonderful but terrifying. The two of you are only of the same bloodline, right?" Alveen was caught off guard by his question.

"Um, yes. What exactly are you suggesting?" She asked, beginning to feel offended.

"Maybe I'm not the only man you've spent the evening with. Maybe Tanilly is your child. You two seem to have enough in common and she looks just like you." Luka's heart hurt as he expressed his thought. Something wasn't adding up.

"Luka." She looked him in the eyes, holding his hands. "I promise, that is not true. None of that is true and I don't know where or when these accusations came to your mind, but I promise you, she is just my niece." She stepped closer to him. As much as she wanted to defend herself and stand up to his outrageous claims, she could only imagine how he must be feeling if those were thoughts he was truly questioning. She needed to reassure him, as his wife, that he had nothing to worry about. "I can't explain any of it, and I understand your frustration. But I need you to be on my team, supporting me right now. I promise I have never been dishonest with you, and you are the only one I have ever even been with." He looked over her face, as if he were trying to find a lie, but it wasn't there. He sighed.

"I apologize. I don't know what came over me. You have to agree though. Something is not normal with you and her." As offended as someone telling her she wasn't normal should have made her, she understood. There was nothing normal about her.

"I know. I wish I knew what was going on, but I have other things that need to be handled right now. Once things calm down we can do further research." He nodded his response to her as he began to walk away towards the entry.

Alveen found Mysti in the hall and informed her of their travel plans. She saw to it that everything was prepared and went off to bring the girls to the entry so they could all leave.

"Mysti, as always, you're welcome to join us." Her friend pondered for a moment. "Irielle is beautiful." She tried convincing her.

"I have wanted to travel more." She bit her lip, thinking on it. "Okay, give me time to pack. The girls and I will be ready to go." Alveen nodded with a smile.

Before leaving, The Queen had to wait in the throne room for the guards to bring her prisoner. Her usual guards, other than Caspian, would be joining them, ensuring her safety with the former Prince unshackled. Caspian stood beside her near the throne as she waited.

"Are you certain you don't want me to come?" He asked for the third time since they had spoken. He looked worried for his Queen's safety. She could feel it.

"Caspian, you are the only one I trust enough to leave my kingdom in your able hands. If this is not a position you desire, then I must know." Her words were caring and Caspian could tell that she understood his emotional predicament. He had vowed to keep her safe, but he hadn't thought about how his current position would prevent him from doing so.

"No, Your Majesty. I am honored to be in this position you've given me. It's a breath of fresh air away from the training grounds. I only wish for you to be safe." His hands were clasped behind his back and his brows were pushed together to visibly show the struggle he was facing. She stopped and crossed her arms, looking up to the white centaur with long blonde hair.

"Caspian?" She asked softly.

"Yes, Your Majesty?"

"Do you trust those that are going on my journey with me?" She asked with a matter of fact look on her face. He nodded with his reply.

"Of course. I handpicked them. They have done a marvelous job even while I was at your side, Your Majesty."

"Then I need you to believe that you have taught them well and that I will remain safe." She smiled. "Do you remember how to summon me?" She asked as she stepped back, waiting to see him show her. "I need to know you can contact me if anything happens to my kingdom or my people. You are the guardian of those most precious to me right now." Her face grew serious. Caspian let out a breath, understanding his importance. He focused for a moment and waved a hand before his face. A cloud appeared in front of Alveen. She waved, accepting the connection. "I will contact you if anything goes wrong. Do you trust me, Sir Caspian?" She saw his face only in the fog that appeared between them, blocking his physical form from her.

"With my life, Queen Alveen." He claimed, placing his fist over his heart and bowing. Alveen repeated the motion, showing mutual respect.

"Then please trust that this is where I need you right now." He nodded, still not certain that he liked that answer, but he did trust her and her instincts. The door burst open, causing them both to lose focus and end the connection. As the fog dissipated around them, Alveen could see her father, walking himself, unshackled and cleaned. She knew now with her new-found ability that he had no ulterior motives, but that didn't make being around him any less awkward.

"We are prepared to depart. Killian, you may follow me." Alveen turned one last time and smiled at Caspian, watching him bow as she exited the room. Killian and his two guards followed.

"Why do you wish for me to travel with you?" Her father asked softly.

"I wish to understand you better, and gain any knowledge you may have of my brother or the powers the Dorcha have been able to access." She said plainly. There was no point in beating around the bush or trying to trick him, honesty was the only way she would handle this situation.

"I've already told you everything I know." His expression was tired and depressing.

"We still have much to discuss." Getting in the last word, Alveen stepped out of the palace, walking down the muddy ramp that would soon grow back into moss, heading towards the stables.

"Your Majesty." Stella and two other guards she had not been introduced to approached her, bowing. "Alicorns and flight harnesses are prepared. It seems everyone is ready for departure. Irielle's Princesses and the attendant are already among the group."

"What of Tanilly?" She asked, realizing she was left out immediately.

"She insisted on riding with you. I told her we would speak with you first." Stella explained. Alveen smiled at this.

"Of course she may." Alveen looked around, realizing all of her alicorns were finally going to get out at the same time. Mysti sat atop Cordelia, Luka on Beastil, Killian would be with a guard on Remia and Allicent waited for his master, The Queen, with a little yet powerful girl by his side.

The Queen took one final look around the group and pulled herself onto Allicent's back, pulling Tanilly up in front of her.

"Are you ready?" She asked with a smile, trying to bring some excitement to the otherwise dreary day. The young girl nodded, excited for lift off. Alveen pushed forward, giving Allicent the sign to run down the cobblestone road and lift into the air. Off the cliffside, the alicorns and centaurs beat their wings and rose into the morning sky. Tanilly leaned against Allicent's neck, holding him tightly as he twisted and turned, ensuring he was flying in the proper direction. Irielle was west of Cosaint, across the Krumvitian Sea.

• • •

Much of the flight was silent, but Tanilly would point out creatures in the water or sky with a smile. She even tried reaching for the clouds multiple times, trailing her fingers through the fog. The little girl that sat in front of her always seemed to bring a warm feeling to Alveen's heart.

As the clouds parted around them, Alveen could feel something off in her gut. The barrier had fallen around Irielle. There was no purple hued electrically charged dome keeping it's citizens protected. The advisor's council would not have been able to reach anyone with Lovisa being dead. Flying closer to the island, Luka and Alveen glanced at each other, trying to warn the other that they both felt uneasy as they passed where the boundary used to stand.

Thick clouds blocked any sun from shining on the island kingdom. It was like the life that had been stolen from Lovisa, was now missing from Irielle as well. Citizens seemed to be missing, no life anywhere. The wind even ceased to move the trees and tall grass along the mountain.

"Alveen? What happened here?" Tanilly asked, tucked between her arms. She could feel something off just as Alveen could.

"That's what we're going to find out." Her guards flew to her side once they realized the eerie feeling in the air.

"Your Majesty. Are you certain you wish to land?" Stella asked with an uncertain expression.

"We must. We need to know what happened or what we are up against." She turned to Luka, addressing him next. "Be prepared for anything." He nodded, relaying the message to his guards as well as they flew closer to the abandoned looking island. Alveen sat tall, radiating confidence as she led her team into an unknown situation.

The group circled the island's numerous times, looking for any sign of life or anything suspicious. The only thing unsettling about their rounds was the lack of, well, anything. the balconies looked abandoned; the trails looked as if they had grown over. The main island at the mountain castle's entrance would be their best bet for landing.

Allicent landed gracefully as the marble pillars surrounding the landing strip raced by. Coming to a steady halt, they looked around the mountain and entrance that seemed to be undisturbed. The towering doors opened outward, revealing the truth behind what had taken place. Luka pushed Beastil forward to see inside before the entrance was revealed to them all. His jaw tensed as he would never be able to unsee what laid before them.

"Alveen, cover her eyes." He raised his voice to his new wife, referring to their adoptive daughter in her arms. He pressed backward, looking at two of his trustworthy protectors. "Guards, take the twins to safety in Loxley now. Have Karolyn summon us when you arrive." He ordered as he rejoined Alveen. "Prepare yourself." He whispered. A few bulgraktan guards remained, along with Stella and a number of cosaintian guards, all braced for the impact of whatever was hiding in the mountain of Irielle. The doors finally reached a point where there was no hiding what they held.

Blood.

Innocent dried blood shed along the stone walls, white marble floors and the faces of Irielle's citizens. Alveen took a quick breath in, but couldn't help looking for familiar faces. She recognized none of them, though that didn't make the massacre any less horrifying. It gave her hope that Irielle's best warrior may still be alive.

"Who could have done this?" The Queen of Cosaint asked. Luka gave her a sideways glance, knowing she knew exactly who. "We should first check the artillery shelter, we need weapons." She pulled the reins, leading her group towards the training grounds.

Stone had been broken and gloomy clouds lingered over the kingdom once draped in warm rays from the suns. The thriving community Alveen found before seized to exist, or so it seemed. The door to the artillery shelter was placed in the side of a hill, cracked slightly ajar. Alveen dismounted from Allicent, handing the reins to Tanilly. Alveen wanted to feel the instincts of a mother, feeling badly for having brought this little girl, but she didn't. Alveen knew the power she was capable of and that she could defend herself if it came down to it, though she wanted to protect her and keep her safe as an older sister would.

● ● ●

"If something happens, you take Allicent. Tell him Loxley and he will go. Do you understand?" She spoke to her niece. Tanilly's eyes began to brighten, the pink hue glowing brighter as she stared at the door ahead.

"Someone is in there. Be careful Alveen." She spoke without blinking. The Queen looked between Tanilly and her destination.

"How do you know?" Alveen had to ask. Tanilly turned towards her, blinking quickly to clear her mind. Her eyes glowed no longer.

"I could see it. Whoever it is, they're injured, but alive. To the right when you enter. Be careful." She whispered, looking around to see if others were listening. Alveen hugged her and winked with a smile as she turned to enter the shelter. Another power unveiled. What abilities didn't this girl have? Luka stood with his daggers, his wrist flicking forward to fling the door open. Alveen tried to remember the layout of the room, preparing for whoever was in there to be on the defense. As she stepped through the door, scanning the walls, many weapons were vacant from their homes. Turning to the right where Tanilly had predicted, was Rowna, her bone snapped in her upper leg, exposed to the air. Streaks of dirt had been wiped across her face.

"Rowna! What happened?" Alveen sped to her side, looking over what had been done to her. Luka continued through the small building with open rooms, preparing for anything to be crouched in corners and ready to attack. He knew the foul play of war, and Rowna could very well be bait.

"Queen Alveen? Do my senses fool me?" She asked with heavy breathes. Before Alveen had a chance to reply, her injured trainer continued, "We saw the barrier drop. We know what happened. It was a trap. They waited outside our northern boundary, taking us by surprise." She explained through her ability to swallow back tears and pain. Alveen looked at her leg, being drawn to it. She was suddenly able to see better, as if a light were turned on. Rowna gasped quietly. It was her eyes glowing. Her magic was coming to the surface.

"Let me help you." Alveen ordered, without turning her gaze away from the blood and bone in front of her. "I need to push it back. Stay strong." Without hesitating, Alveen pulled her leg and pushed down on the exposed bone. Shallow cries and deep gasps for air escaped Rowna's lips, slowly fading as she watched her ally Queen wave her hands over her leg, now surrounded in a white light. It felt cool against her skin, like ice water swirled around it, mending the imperfection. Her eyes grew wide as the pain disappeared. When the light faded, Alveen stood, extending a hand.

"How.." the executive trainer couldn't find the words to ask how she had the ability she did. Though magic was certainly a part of their healing process, it was never that quick or painless and it was never an experience like that.

"Let's just say I have access abilities that allow me to help in dire situations." Alveen answered, leaving it at that as she began asking questions. "Who attacked Irielle? The Dorcha?"

"Yes. All of them by the looks of it. The first wave of them were the syragons. With us being so ill prepared they…" she paused as the memory of the monsters thrashing through bodies was still so raw in her mind, "slaughtering" she said through tears. "slaughtering everyone. The main entrance. It looked like.." She tried to go on.

"We saw. We know." Alveen stated with understanding. "How did you get over here?" Rowna now sat on a hill in the still grass.

"I called to the warriors. We were on our way to the shelter when the barrier first began to drop. I had accumulated a few weapons and ran back to defend the entrance. When I saw what happened I couldn't believe they had reached it so quickly. As I was about to follow through the mountain, another wave came. More of them. I've never seen so many. They flew past us, leaving us all for dead. I pulled myself into the shelter, knowing I couldn't continue to fight, seeing so few survivors left." Tears still streamed down her face as the battle scene replayed in her eyes as if she were reliving it again. Alveen squatted down, placing Rowna's arm over her shoulder and lifting her off the ground and led her outside of the shelter.

"Wait, syragons? They are able to be on land again?" Alveen's eyes widened. She had told people this would happen again and everyone thought it had been a fluke or a one-time ritual. "Rowna. Are they still here? Where are they all?"

"I don't know. I heard them all and then I blacked out on and off. I thought for certain a syragon would have sniffed out the blood. When I heard the entrance doors open, I expected it to be them."

"How many tribe members crossed the border?" Stella asked from behind, trying to prepare herself and co-guards for what they would face.

"None. You don't understand. They were *all* syragons. An army of them."

"Apparently the whole rule of a double moon is no longer in play for the unnatural creatures." Luka sighed, thinking back to all of his research. "I don't understand it. I thought for certain it was a ritual or spell last time that gave them this ability. I don't see Zakarian or Malika being strong enough to pull anything like this off so soon." A scoff and chuckle came from behind them.

"I don't think a ritual or ceremony would have been strong enough to allow them on land for a night. It would need to be something that affected each one individually." It was Killian who spoke now. His eyes didn't show amusement, but he wore a small smile.

"I thought you told us everything you knew?" Alveen asked, approaching her father.

"I assumed you knew more. I apologize. I expect you are not going to like what I have to tell you then." He sighed, dismounting as well, still surrounded by guards. He looked between those who guarded him, his long hair pulled back neatly in a ponytail. It was the first time she really noticed that he looked like the Prince he once was. His peridot eyes stared at her, reminding her of her grandmother. "Those creatures are able to be manipulated by the creator of them, the moon has nothing to do with it." He revealed.

"It must have some role, otherwise why would the sorceress have kept them at bay for so long between double moons?" Rowna asked, confused, much like those around her.

"To sell the lie." He stated simply. "She used them for many things on land, it was just not attacking. They dug tunnels, they were her personal security, those such things that weak and nearly dead creatures couldn't perform well." He explained, astonished that they hadn't figured that out.

"All of our research claimed what we thought to be true." Luka stated.

"Because that is what all of the scholars believed." Killian replied bluntly. "They were controlled by her and now that she is gone…"

"Zakarian controls them?" Alveen answered, thinking she knew the way it would work.

"No, my dear. They are controlled by no one. We must find a way to finish their line. They now have minds of their own. Just as when the original sorceress died, her creations became free of manipulation. Lyra didn't like it when they didn't listen to her. She murdered them all but used many of her weak and dying tribe members to transform into her own minions. I'm going to assume Zakarian has tried to do the same. Though Lyra created so many, I don't see how it would be possible for Zakarian and Malika to kill them all. I have no doubt there are some that still remain unleashed." His detail of the creatures seemed vast. As Killian spoke, Alveen experienced a mix of emotions. All the research and answers that Luka and Alveen had thought they knew, was wrong. All their theories shut down in seconds. She riffled through the information she now had.

"Okay, this changes things but either way, we need to get inside and find out if anyone else survived." She planned out loud as she pulled herself back up on Allicent's back behind Tanilly, who had sat there quietly.

Alveen quickly contacted Caspian to inform him of their situation though he fought her to let him lead troops there, or to inform Viktor and Willow so they could send back up, Alveen refused, letting him know so far all they've found is dead bodies. There was no reason to send an army to defend them against that. They had no idea if anyone was even in the castle. Caspian huffed disapprovingly as Alveen got in the final word, telling him to wait for her call.

They cautiously walked back to the entrance doors, examining everything they could on their way. The balconies that wrapped around the mountain held no one and there was so little movement that it cast an even more unnerving ambiance over the kingdom. The Queen turned to her trusted guard. "Stella, I need you to take Tanilly to Loxley. I do not want her around all of this. She must be protected." Stella seemed to be less than thrilled with having to leave, but in her heart she understood the importance of this young girl. She would rule over Cosaint one day. The final heir to the Cosaint and Bulgrakta throne.

"Alveen, don't make me leave. I can help. You know I can." The young girl proclaimed stubbornly.

"I know, I know." Alveen said as she ran her hand across her niece's cheek. "I know you are so strong and powerful, but I need you protected. I cannot risk anything happening to you. Someday you will be by our side during these incidents, but for now, I need you safe. Do you understand?" She explained with a pained expression. Alveen wanted Tanilly by her and Luka, knowing they could protect her, but in this case she wasn't certain she could. Tanilly sighed deeply and walked towards Stella, hoping on her back. "Tanilly?" The Queen called. "You know I love you, right?" The girl smiled. No one had ever been as kind or protective of her as the new Queen, her aunt.

"I love you too Aunt Alveen." She said with a grin. Alveen was taken aback by the title. She had never called her that before.

Tanilly shot her arm out and clenched her fist, followed by a shrill scream behind them. Half a dozen syragons twisted on the ground as Tanilly drove her magic through them, soon bursting into flames leaving only the ash of their corpses behind. Luka looked between the young girl and the pile of ash before them. She just killed. For the first time, she took life, even if it was that of an evil creature.

"Tanilly. Are you okay?" Alveen had jumped off Allicent and walked over to hug her. She stared into her eyes, searching for a sign of hardness.

"I'm okay. I told you, I can help. I have learned control. I will do whatever it takes to protect the kingdoms." A tear fell from her face. The reality of taking a life was sinking in. "I just killed them. They use to be good." The tears still flowed down her cheeks but emotion did not escape her lips.

"It's okay. You were defending us. They were transformed into something evil. Unsavable." Luka was at their side, pulling Tanilly in for a comforting hug.

"It will never be easy. You should not have had to experience this at such a young age." He explained as he rubbed her back. "Will you please leave with Stella now?" He asked, tilting her head up so he could read her eyes.

"No. I want to stay and help. I'm going to be Queen someday. I need to be prepared." She explained. For such a young creature, she was determined. Luka looked between her and his wife, who stood nearby not blinking as she thought about how to proceed.

"My Queen?" He asked, calling for her opinion on the matter. She looked around. It was getting dark, they needed to begin their raid through the castle soon.

● ● ●

"Stella?" She turned to the centaur who had stood by quietly at attention.

"Yes, Your Majesty?"

"Protect her at all costs. She's coming with us." Alveen walked off, pulling herself onto Allicent. "We need to get through the castle, quick. Night falls soon." She nudged the alicorn with her heel and headed off towards the entrance with the Bulgraktan guards. Luka placed Tanilly on Stella's back.

"You protect Stella too, okay?" He told his adoptive daughter. "Be safe, Princess." She wasn't used to being called that yet.

Catching up to Alveen; Luka, Stella, Killian and the entourage of guards slowly walked through the entrance, stepping over bodies that laid mangled along the marble floor. Alveen wanted to keep looking away, but the fire within her knew that if she looked, she would become more determined. She would remember their faces and she would never forget why she fought this war.

Alveen remembered the basic layout of the mountain palace, leading her group down the halls that wrapped the outside of the throne room. Beyond the echoing of the alicorns hooves, their elven senses picked up on a subtle clicking against the marble floor, in beat with their steps. Alveen glanced at Luka. Everyone could hear it now as the clicking grew closer to them. Everyone pressed up against the wall, waiting to see what would greet them.

• • •

The King of Bulgrakta gripped his sword, waiting alongside the corridor. It became clear that the clicking was footsteps. He could now hear the weight of something dragging on the floor only just slightly further back. Stepping out into their view was an average sized syragon, its scales covered in dirt. Blood was dried along its arms and chest. Before inspecting much further, Luka swung his sword at the soft abdomen of the beast, catching it off guard. As the syragon turned its head, it was already too late. Luka's blade dripped with the blood of the unnatural creature, disconnecting the entire top half of its body. Luka watched it drop to the ground with its hefty weight as the dark liquid flowed from its veins and pooled around its body.

Tanilly stared, unable to take her eyes off of it. Alveen looked her over for a moment. The young girl took a deep breath in and then met her eyes. She would be able to handle this and it would make her stronger when she led battle someday, if she ever had to.

"We must keep moving." Luka walked out from the wall heading down the corridor where the monster had just emerged, only to be met by a crowded hall. On both sides, syragons stood now staring down at what seemed to be their commander. Ferocious growls and roars burst out all at once, echoing through the marbled structure. "Alveen! Tanilly! Right now would be a great time for your aid." Luka prepared himself, ready to slice his blade through as many dorcha that it took to regain the Irielle throne. Alveen tried to summon her magic but before she had enough control over it, a cloud

• • •

formed in the hallway, blocking everyone's view of the oncoming danger. The aroma of wet earth clung tight to their senses. Their talons seized clicking against the floor and the dragging of tails came to a halt as coughing ensued and bodies fell.

Stella looked back at The Princess, her eyes shining a magnificent white light, her veins glowing royal blue as she embraced her power to defend herself and her family. She began breathing heavy and blinked, cutting off her hold on her magic. As the smoke cleared, none of the enemies were left standing. Looking down on them, the bodies had shriveled and dried to a crisp but the air had become heavy with humidity. The Princess had drawn out all the water from their bodies.

"Well… there's that way too." Killian spoke. He had not seen much for their magic abilities, but his granddaughter impressed him. He spoke confidently, but his eyes reflected his fear for the power the young girl beside him held within her grasp.

Alveen motioned forward after she saw to it that Tanilly was alright. Allicent stepped over the dead corpses, their flesh looking as though it would be blown into dust. The hallways still echoed with the battle cry of oncoming enemies. Alveen gripped her sword tight as she summoned her magic. With an exhale, the sword felt like it became an extension of her body, allowing the magic to travel along the steel blade like vines in a haste to reach to end of the limb they crawled upon. Her hearing became enhanced, more than she had ever realized.

● ● ●

With each footfall nearing them, she anticipated the creature's movements.

Entering the next corridor, she swung her sword melodically, ripping with ease through the flesh and bones of the unnatural beings. Heads became detached from the shoulders, limbs were lost and as if the magic heated the blade she swung, it repeatedly plunged through her opponents.

Stella and other guards had stepped into position but before they could swing their own weapons, there were none left to defeat. Alveen sat splattered with blood, her blade illuminating a bluish hue as it pulsed with the magic. They stood in bewilderment at the warrior Queen.

Approaching the throne room, they could hear nothing. They all dismounted as they began to break across the threshold of the room where Queen Lovisa once sat.

With a fast beating heart in her chest, Alveen pushed forward, leading the group into unknown danger. They hadn't yet walked into the room but she could make out certain details. The skylights high above allowed in little light. Rays of light shined down on the Irielle throne enough to illuminate the weak, brittle face of her brother, and the crazed woman by his side that after a moment, she recognized as Malika.

"Stella? Killian?" Alveen could hear Luka speaking. "Take Tanilly and go. Loxley should be safe." Luka had commanded them to leave with their adoptive daughter. She would be a great force on their side, but these were her parents, and she shouldn't have to see them this way.

Walking into the throne room, Alveen and Luka both had the same mind set. This would not be one where Zakarian was allowed to speak and converse with them, his people were going to die for what they did to the solas kingdoms.

As soon as they entered, swarms of syragons surrounded them. Back to back they would fight as much as possible. Their guards still entered from the corridor, taking stance and measuring up their opponents with haste before swinging the first sword. Talons beat along the marble floors, low growls rumbled in the chests of the dozens of beasts that began to enclose around them. Guards who once would have shook in their boots now stood strong, ready to tear down the entire army of monsters.

With a grunt from one of Luka's guards, a head detached from one of the syragons near him. he had apparently been on the same page- there will be no talking. The head that rolled on the floor didn't phase the others at all, but within moments the sorceress created army braced for attack.

Alveen loosened her grip, feeling the hilt of her blade find its comfortable place in her palm as her legs tensed, ready to jump. With a swing upward, the nearest syragon was split open, its dark innards pouring out. As if it were the signal they all waited for, the battle began. Claws and talons scraped through the air. Blades followed them as their group slowly began to push outward. Luka swung his weapon around his head, ripping apart the first layer of beasts in his path.

A clench of her fist and the scale covered necks snapped and slimy centaur like bodies dropped to the floor. Alveen performed another flawless maneuver swinging her weapons.

The guards were separated from Luka and Alveen when a swarm of syragons pressed in on them. Alveen became distracted, trying to keep watch on them and protecting them. With the split second she looked to the others, her blade was flung from her hands and she was knocked onto the marble floor. Killian lay next to her. Luka had been held back by three of the creatures, forced to his knees in front of Zakarian and Malika, or the new twisted, deranged versions of them anyways.

"Ah father. So nice to see you've come to join us."

"I've done no such thing. I loved your mother for what she was born as, and hoped I could save her, but she was terrible to others and power and blood became all she desired. I no longer loved who she had become. You are a spitting image." The broken prince pushed himself up onto his knees when he spoke. He reached over and pulled Alveen up, giving her the push she needed to pull herself into a squat position.

"I'll take that as a compliment." Zakarian replied with a grim smile. "And you, sister." he stood, walking towards them. "I gave you the chance to join this. Since I had denounced the throne I realized, I really do want to rule over people. What a better way to rule then by taking a kingdom. The Dorcha surely don't have a stationary residence, but I think this place will do just fine." He looked at her with pity, though she couldn't figure out why.

• • •

"I still decline. You have started a war you will not be able to finish." She proclaimed with fire in her eyes. "You've murdered so many and gone against the foundation of magic yielding. Do not expect us to stand by and allow you to   take over an ally kingdom. You will be rid of one way or another."

"That's not the way it looks from here." He paced in front of them. Alveen looked back, her guards had been taken captive as well. She supposed it was better than being murdered on the spot. She thought of Tanilly, hoping she made it out of the kingdom safe. As if on cue, she heard her voice. She was talking with Stella, who wore a triumphant smile. They were flying back towards the mountain castle that held her currently. *No. Turn around. Go the other way.* Alveen became frustrated. Somehow, she had to defeat Zakarian and his army of misshapen half breeds. She analyzed her situation, just as she had in her trials. She took too long. Before she was able to react, a syragon lifted her up off the ground by her throat. She searched deep in her veins for her magic, but it was gone. Like it had done before. Something was blocking it. Pressure grew stronger on her throat, cutting off her air. Drool hung from the large underbitten jaw jammed full with serrated fangs. It's eyes, barren white, watching with pleasure as she struggled. The claws at the end of the beast's fingers dug into her skin. Blood trailed down her neck as she fought with her physical strength. She could only hear Luka's angry wail beyond faded hearing as her vision began to blur. Flames burst forth from the throne room door and poured down from the skylights. *Flames?* Alveen thought to herself. Where are those coming from?

• • •

Alveen dropped to the floor with a thud as the monster before her combusted, the flames lapping along the scales from the innards of the creature. Luka ran to her side. "Alveen? Answer me." His voice was stressed and panicked. She couldn't die like this. The great Queen Alveen would not be taken down by being strangled. He shook her as he continually tried to wake her. Alveen could hear him, but her vision was black. She could hear the explosions happening all around the mountain.

"Can you heal her?" Luka was still speaking, but it was to someone new who had joined them. Alveen still couldn't move and couldn't see. Her magic still blocked from her. A slimy palm covered her throat. A few words were exchanged as Alveen was able to regain her sight. Blurry at first, but soon the golden eyes of her husband entered her vision, along with Shaya, the mermaid she became friends with back in palace bay, on the back of an alicorn she didn't recognize.

"Wha-?" Alveen didn't get a word out before she was lifted onto the back of Beastil with Luka, flying out of the skylight in the mountain, passing dull hued layers of rock and dirt. She held onto Luka's waist as she looked around to see what had transpired.

A group of Cosaintian and Bulgraktan warriors were flying away from Irielle while the mountain began to shake and crack and fall in upon itself back on the island. She looked up to Luka, who had already been staring at her.

"It seems Caspian didn't listen to your commands, Your Majesty." He smiled. She tried sitting up and looking around.

• • •

Caspian flew by their side, his armored body and wings looking like a part of him. He gave her an apologetic glance. She smiled. He knew she needed help and was too stubborn and impatient to ask and wait for it. Thankfully, he knew her well and called upon a group of warriors for back up. The Bulgraktan train was in the air along side them further out. That's how they made it there so quickly.

"I will have to reward him for having such good instincts." She leaned against him, her throat still in pain. "They cut off my magic again." she said quietly, though his elf senses could still hear her.

"I assumed as much. Thankfully Tanilly wasn't far out of Irielle when she saw the approaching army. She set off the distractions allowing us to get out."

"Shaya. How did she heal me? Why was she even brought along?" She asked so confused by her presence.

"You'll have to ask her when we get back." The remainder of the flight was silent, Alveen slept against Luka's chest, one arm wrapped around her protectively and the other hand gripping the reins.

~Chapter X~
Counteractive Magic

The ceiling was familiar. Branches twisted and turned, creating designs that she could only just recall through her foggy memory. Thick fabric hung on the bed canopy wrapping around the posts. After a moment it finally clicked. She was in her old room. Alveen sat up, slowly searching the room. A figure sat on the couch, staring into the flames. Her husband. Hearing her begin to move around, he looked back, relief covering his features.

"How did i..." Alveen began. The last she remembered she had been on an alicorn. How did she not wake when they landed? Luka stood and came to her side. It took her by surprise to see he was wearing a black t-shirt and pajama pants. What time was it?

"I brought you here. I thought you'd like something familiar after the intense day we experienced." She did appreciate that. He lifted the covers and moved close to her, wrapping his arms around her. She didn't argue as she snuggled into his shirt after kissing his cheek.

• • •

"How long have I been sleeping?" She wondered.

"A little over forty-eight hours. We arrived late last night. The healers said because you had used so much magic, draining your energy in the process that because your body was healing, it could be a couple days. As usual you are resilient." He smiled, kissing her head.

"I still feel so tired."

"I bet you do. It's evening now, you may as well try getting as much sleep as you can." She didn't argue as she began to drift off again. She didn't toss and turn in the darkness. Exhaustion still draped over her in a weighted blanket she simply didn't have the strength to move.

Morning came and she woke before Luka. After almost three full days of sleep, she still felt tired and fatigued. Her body kept telling her to return to bed, but her mind fought to stay awake. She forced herself to get dressed for the day. An outfit already laid out for her on the back of a chair by the fireplace. It was appreciated that they had prepared for that, so she didn't have to walk through the palace in clothes she slept in. A knock echoed from the door. Luka jumped up quickly going to the door. Alveen was shocked and amused at his maneuver.

"I could have answered that." Alveen said from the chair. Luka pushed his eyebrows together confused, looking back to the bed.

"I assumed you were still sleeping." He smiled. "But I should have guessed you'd be up. Unfortunately, I don't think you're allowed to be up and about yet." As he pulled the door back, two healers walked in alongside Caspian.

"Banri Alveen." He bowed deeply. "I'm pleased to see you're awake. How are you feeling?" Caspian's platinum hair was pulled back in a ponytail.

"I feel okay, I suppose. My mind is foggy and I'm exhausted. I have many questions." She paused trying to recall everything that happened. "What is the status of the kingdoms?"

"Irielle is still in the grasps of Zakarian and Malika. Syragon numbers have dwindled for the time being." He looked her over again before addressing the healers.

"Check her over please." Caspian ordered them politely. Concern filled his green eyes.

"I'm fine, really. I just over exerted myself is all." She looked around. Luka stood with his arms crossed staring at her. "Shaya." She said suddenly off track. "Shaya healed me." Alveen proclaimed to the already informed faces before her. "How?"

"A newly discovered secret she shared with us. Mermaids have a unique power to undo the damage of a syragon, assuming there is something left to save. They are the light and healing to the darkness and damage that was created from them. They cannot resurrect the dead, but if a syragon is causing distress, or a magic blockage perhaps, that is something that they can counteract." Caspian tried explaining, "She said her and the other mermaids scavenged the wreckage from the battle underwater. They found many books, spell books to be exact. They decided to go through them to see if anything would be helpful to putting an end to this war when she found the spell for blocking an elves magic. She remembered hearing about it and decided it was for us to decide what to do with the information. Very good timing I might add, as they came to us with this information only shortly after you left. When you explained the situation in Irielle, we took flight."

"How exactly does a syragon block magic? I've fought many with magic before."

"Only original syragons. From the first litter. The mermaids also collected baskets of scales, after running multiple tests, we've determined they are used to create that blockage. They were embedded into your mask and King Viktor's crown."

"So how did you know I would be in danger? How did you know to bring her?" Alveen questioned with suspicion.

"I didn't. I just knew if you were against one again, which you said there was a good likely hood of, she was the only thing that could save you. I played it safe and followed my instincts, Your Majesty." Alveen looked her advisor over.

"I suppose that is why you have the position you do." The healers checked her vitals and did multiple tests to determine her health.

"I would advise another day of rest, Your Majesty. You overdid it. Your body needs to recover." They told her before leaving without another words.

"You heard her. I'll take care of things until then." Caspian reassured her. Luka walked up to his wife, but before he could talk, she spoke up.

"Have you spoken to Queen Karolyn? She has the twins. How are they?"

"Safe. Queen Karolyn has taken them both in." Alveen nodded in understanding. They made it safely.

"We need to end this. Once and for all." she concluded quietly. "My brother is gone, the real Zakarian anyways. He would not have hesitated to let them kill me, or his own daughter, or any of the others. So I will not hesitate to take their lives either."

"What are you saying, Your Majesty?" He asked with a small grin peeking through his thick, dark facial hair.

"I'm saying we're going to need every warrior and citizen in Beannithe. One final battle to solidify the peace we need. We've tried multiple times. We need something that is going to solidify the end of that tribe and the evil they bring to our world."

"You still need to recover."

"I can strategize from my chamber. If you will summon the others, we can officially declare war."

"Of course, Your Grace." Luka had been ready to end this fight for a long time but no one had ever stood by his aggressive tactics until now. Everyone always wanted to be the better people, but all that was doing was getting innocents murdered and stripping away the peace they once knew.

Luka summoned each of the leaders from their ally kingdoms, one at a time. Alveen was the only one who could summon them all at once and she was restricted from using even the smallest amount of magic. Every leader agreed that it was time. Time to put aside their ideals of being the better people in order to protect their citizens and kingdoms.

"So it is settled. We finish this war." Banri Alveen declared with a smile on her face and she looked over papers and maps strewn about the bed in front of her. The plans had been set, the strategies discussed back and forth and they were certain, this time, they would end this war once and for all.

"Lead us well Banri." Queen Karolyn commented before disappearing.

"Are you ready for this?" Luka asked his wife. Her hair was pulled up and she was still in her pajamas, but she just declared war on the entire tribe that stood against her. A fire burned in her eyes and Luka could not look away from the fierce woman he fell in love with.

"More than ever." She responded, still going over everything before her.

"You need rest, my beautiful, fierce, battle ready Queen." He said quietly, crawling into bed next to her. He folded everything together and put them in the nightstand.

"Fine. But tomorrow, I need to go to the armory."

She was happy to be out of her sleeping clothes and in her form fitting jeans, brown leather boots with buckles and straps, burgundy long sleeve shirt with a matching brown leather vest and to finish her outfit, her golden crown of embedded leaves and vines to rest on her loose curls. Luka was still sleeping. She was always awake before him, but she didn't mind because it gave her time to refocus in silence in the morning. Out her bedroom door she silently went, her sights set on a very specific weapon.

The armory was dark and quiet, but her elven ears could still hear conversations happening outside in the training yard and her eyes adjusted with no trouble at all. Her footfalls were ghost-like on the solid ground as she made her way passed rows of training weapons. In the back was a wooden wall with swords and archery equipment organized in a very particular order. Quickly searching the wall, her heightened senses found what she was looking for in only moments. The sword she wielded while charging through the corridors of Irielle's mountain castle. She remembered the teal color it glowed, much like her own eyes, when it harnessed the magic that she allowed to pour out of herself while in the heat of battle. She wondered how it could do something like that, and if there were a way to forge a weapon similar in order to keep her from using all her energy in the upcoming war she intended on declaring.

Enough was enough. This constant state of fear and living within kingdom walls needed to be over. The citizens of Beannithe deserved to be able to travel around their countryside and experience the world beyond their own barriers. The Dorcha tribe was dwindling and their power was growing weaker. With the final Sorceress gone, there should have been no reason why the life long war was still happening. It had turned from opposing sides because of different beliefs in the magic system into a pure and raw form of evil that fought for no reason other than to bring death and destruction. No more. Not under Banri Alveen. Her legacy would be one of strength, assertiveness and getting things done. This Queen will be known for her backbone and for her ability to make change happen, including ending a war that had gone on for far too long.

The thoughts ignited a passion in her that released magic. The sword before her began to glow as it had previously. She watched with a slight smile as she felt the presence of another approaching.

"Your Majesty?" Sir Caspian entered the armory. He stood near her, watching the sword.

"What is it about that sword that allows it to harness my magic? What makes it different?" She asked quietly to the silent centaur by her side.

"I could not tell you. However, Elkin may be able to tell you. He is the finest blacksmith and weapons creator in history. He helped create many of Krumvites magic infused weapons as well."

"Elkin, you said?" She asked confirming his name, thinking of why she had never met him before.

"Yes, Your Majesty."

"Is he in Cosaint? May I speak with him, immediately?" Her eyes had not left the sword.

"Yes, of course. I believe he is out on the field now. I'll retrieve him at once, Banri Alveen." The thudding of his hooves against the stone floor faded as he galloped out of the armory, leaving The Queen to her thoughts. Was it the metal? Was it how the blade was formed, or who it was formed by? Possibly something else entirely.

"Ah, Your Majesty! What an honor to finally meet you." A middle-aged warlock walked in alongside Caspian, kneeling to her in respect and rising. He was bald, with dark eyes, his stature rather short. She looked him over, wondering how she had missed him all this time. "Sir Caspian said you wished to speak to me."

"Yes. I don't know how we hadn't met yet but i'm glad we finally are. I have a question about this sword here." She extended her arm towards it, concealing her magic to see what he knew first.

"Ah, unique, isn't it? We found it in the woods, believe it or not. Only a short time ago. The hilt and the blade itself contain inscriptions. the language is similar to ours but I don't quite understand it. I have even called upon some of the scholars from the palace library. No one can figure it out. What is it about this blade that interests you, Your Majesty?" Alveen dropped her mind barrier allowing her magic to flow through her veins. Her eyes began to glow, along with the blade. Elkin stood back, staring in wonder and admiration.

"I would like to know how it is able to do this, and if it can be recreated. I was able to harness my magic and control it much easier when I wield that blade in Irielle."

"I have never seen anything like this before." He leaned closer to the blade, "The words. They're illuminating." his gaze turned quizzical, "How is this possible?" He ran over to a desk nearby, grabbing a small journal. "I've been working on something." He disappeared into a side room, returning with a tall twisted branch, the top held a double axe head. Upon inspecting further, the branch was engraved with the same symbols. Vines grew around them. "See if this will do the same thing. I've spent so much time staring at this sword trying to figure it out that I copied all the symbols down. Alveen looked to Caspian who nodded in approval.

"It is beautiful, I will admit that."

"Thank-you, Your Grace. I take great pride in my work." With a deep breath in and a long breath out, the sparks began to flow again. A breeze blew in from the exterior door, surrounding her and tossing her curls to one direction. The air began to wrap around the branch in her grasp, swirling passed the symbols and lighting them up in a rhythmic pattern. Caspian and Elkin stood back, watching as their Queen lay claim to a weapon that seemed to be created for her. The wind dissipated, leaving the new weapon glowing.

"I think this will do just fine, Elkin." She smiled, feeling a power inside of her. Something felt so right about the staff in her grip.

"I... yes of course." His breath quickened, "It worked. I don't know what it is but, it worked. That was just a silly project of mine."

"Well, your time and work will be compensated well Elkin. Do you think you can make a dagger with similar inscriptions?"

"I will do my very best." She nodded and left the armory with her massive weapon, though she carried it with ease despite the weight of the top.

Throwing the doors open, she felt unstoppable. Luka was awake now, dressed and in front of the fire, sipping on a steaming beverage. His eyebrow rose as he turned and watched Alveen walk into the room.

"Where is Tanilly?" She asked in her usual tone.

"Probably in class, where she belongs on a day like this." He stated as though it should be obvious. "You don't even know what day it is, do you?" He chuckled. She had been asleep for over two full days.

"I really don't" She laughed at herself. He looked her over with a grin. "What?" She asked him.

"Nothing, you just look good. Love the new weapon, by the way." He leaned back with his arm across the top of the couch, turned toward her with his drink in hand.

"You will not believe this." She smiled as she exhaled and displayed the connection between her and the double-edged blade and staff.

"It's like the sword." He stated, surprised.

"Yes, I'm seeing if he can create a dagger for Tanilly." She stated quietly. They hadn't talked about her fighting yet, but she knew her niece could handle herself, and protect others while doing it. She may have been young, but she was more powerful than even Alveen.

"You want Tanilly to fight?" He asked calmly. Looking her in the eyes, he searched for how sure she was of this.

"I do. Though I want to protect her, I strongly believe no one can protect her like she can herself. We have both witnessed her ability to fight. If she has a weapon that can help harness her magic, then she is an asset to us." Luka's protective instincts kicked in, but he knew she was right. The girl was unique.

"If she fights, she gets her own guards. I want her surrounded by our people and no one else's." He gave her the ultimatum.

"Agreed. She will be with Stella and others that we trust. I have a plan though as I do not wish for her to be the front line."

"I'm listening."

~ CHAPTER XI ~
WAR FOR PEACE

Alveen knew she had to address her people. She needed to talk to them first hand. Caspian had called the kingdom together for her in front of the palace. Alveen wore her fur cloak, her golden crown and her casual outfit underneath, still wielding the staff. Luka stood beside her, his golden crown on his rough styled hair, a black fur cloak resting atop his shoulders. The air had warmed in recent days, preparing for the changing of seasons but the brisk wind hung around. He reached out his hand, grabbing hold of hers. She smiled without looking at him, taking a deep breath in. The staff began to glow as she allowed her emotions to flow into it.

They walked to the top of the ramp at the palace entry, stopping to wait for the applause to seize after they were announced.

"Cosaintians. You deserve to hear this from my own lips. The Dorcha Tribe has taken over Irielle. They murdered Queen Lovisa and took advantage of the time the Irielle barrier was down." Gasps and chatting began, "I don't know about all of you, but I am fed up. I am furious with the amount of innocent lives taken. I am DONE being the better people when it has done nothing but cause us all hurt. I have arranged with the other Monarchs and they agree. We declare WAR on the Dorcha. For a final battle will take place and we will win our peace back." Citizens nodded, you could see in their eyes that they too were fed up. They were tired of waiting for monarchs to make the right call, but finally one had. "I ask you, as Banri of your kingdom, to fight alongside us. I will not order anyone to do so. We will need people to stay behind to defend the kingdom should anything happen." She paused for effect, giving them a second to hear her words. "Plans are made already. We will reconvene this evening for those of you who wish to join us, for in the morning we fly for the dark lands north of Loxley and Irielle." She lifted her staff, glowing. It became a symbol of hope for her citizens. They had been hurt much like she had, losing people for only selfish and evil desires to be fulfilled. They were tired of feeling powerless.

"You are much better at this then I would have thought." Luka whispered as they turned to walk into the palace.

"I was pretty good, wasn't I?" She laughed. "Do you think they'll fight?" She asked with a worried expression.

"Yes. without hesitation. They feel the pain you speak of, I could see it. They want to feel like they have the power to do something and you are giving them that." She hoped he was right. They met in the conference room outside the Banri's chambers with Caspian and the other monarchs on call as they made a strategic plan they could present to anyone that met them in the Armory.

Evening came and with a heavy sigh Alveen made her way through the corridors and out to the armory where Caspian would be waiting with anyone willing to join. A solid black gown with long sleeves and a high neck was her ensemble. Her golden leaf encrusted crown sat on her head of loose curls and a sleeveless, floor length fur cape wrapped around her figure. She kept her expectations low to avoid disappointment if the turnout was not all she hoped. She focused on the sound of her own boots meeting the stone ground and the swishing of her dress as she walked.

"Stand for your Banri." A voice echoed as she approached the door. Her thoughts ordered the heavily detailed iron doors open without her needing to lift a finger. The smells of fire and iron wrapped around her, giving her a boost of courage and strength. Though she felt confident, she was taken back by how many citizens filled the dark room before her. The warm glow of the wall sconces and candles illuminated the features of both citizens she had met and those she didn't know. Shoulder to shoulder citizens stood, ready to fight with her. They applauded her arrival. It seemed as though they were already inspired and encouraged and ready for battle as they hollered fiercely.

"I'm impressed. I wasn't expecting so many." She whispered as she approached Sir Caspian who stood at the head of the room with a wall full of axes and weapons behind him.

"You inspire them, Your Majesty." he smiled. She calmed her heart beat as she addressed them all now.

"Words cannot describe my gratitude to you all. I am proud of each of you for taking a stand and for being fed up with the way this life is. You deserve better and tomorrow, we will fight for the life you all deserve. A life where your loved ones are only taken from old age or illness and not from attacks from heartless enemies." She scanned over faces, taking in their expressions of agreement. "Sir Caspian will lead the majority of this meeting as he is in charge of our strategy of approach. You will all do well to listen. Ask questions if you have them, I understand you have all been given the basic training, but this will take on much more than that. I do not want anyone leaving here confused." They all nodded. Alveen turned, the fur cape twirling behind her as she sat in a nearby chair as Sir Caspian stood to explain their plan of action.

When the meeting convened, the Generals and Captains of the army stayed around to answer questions for those too shy to speak aloud to the group. In the eyes of every man and woman there, she saw hope. She also saw fear being swallowed by their frustration and the opportunity they were finally given.

"Walk with me, My Banri?" Sir Caspian requested, holding his arm out to her. With a quick smile, she stood and let the head of her army walk her through thick crowds of citizens. "They respect you. I've never seen anything like it to be honest." He said through the hum of the crowd around them.

"What do you mean? Haven't they always respected their monarchs?"

"Yes. To an extent. There was still something between them. As if they were not high enough class or good enough to interact with them. I've seen the confidence and love and hope that flashes in their eyes when you walk among them and talk with them. I figured it would not be a bad way to end the evening."

"I will never understand that. Perhaps my being away was for the best, don't you think?" She asked the centaur beside her.

"I do. Your view of the world and relationships had given a new light to this place. To all of Beannithe, dare I say."

"I don't feel as though I have that much of an impact." She whispered. "I do love being around them. This village warms my heart. I just feel home when I'm walking these streets." She explained, glancing around at the street lights and trees swaying in the evening breeze. It was a brisk evening. She pulled her fur cape around her to keep the chill out.

After stopping by a few local shops, she spent time speaking with families about what they will do once they win back the ability to do and see more than just the inside of their kingdom. With the constant threat of the Dorcha, the barriers had been put in place to keep the kingdoms safe, unfortunately that also meant the citizens of each kingdom were much like prisoners in their own homes, unable to leave and see the world. The kingdoms had each done an exceptional job at providing everything they needed and plenty to do. The only traveling and adventuring happening was by the monarchs under heavy guard though. Many spoke of visiting Bulgrakta.

"It is truly beautiful. I hope to one day see you there." She stated. It was time for her evening to end. Early in the morning, they would be off. She needed her rest if she was going to lead and army into battle tomorrow. She waved and smiled as she took Caspian's arm, who led her to the palace.

"Thank-you for being my second this evening." She said to him as he placed a fist over her heart and bowed.

"Always, Your Majesty. I will see you in the morning." She let out a deep breath as she went back to her chambers where Luka was waiting.

"There she is. I began to think you may be starting a riot and leave early." He was sitting at the fireplace with a book in hand. His brown eyes reflecting the flames as they always did. She could get used to this view.

"Mmm, and miss a chance to spend time with you before I fly off to war? Never." She leaned down and kissed him before changing for bed.

"Are you ready?" He asked her.

"Of course. This evening made me even more certain of my decision. These citizens need their lives back and their freedom. They need to not have to live in fear." He smiled as his wife spoke so passionately.

"Here." He handed her a mug of steaming tea. The cinnamon scent familiar to her twirled in smokey bands before her face. "I figured you would have some difficulty getting to sleep. You need your rest."

"What and you can just fall asleep with no trouble the evening before heading to war?" She asked with a smile.

"No, I already drank mine." He winked, pointing to his empty mug. It wasn't long before she drifted off, preparing herself for a day of travel.

She rose before the sun, hoping to let Luka rest for just a little while longer while she pulled on her battle apparel. Staring into the flames of the fireplace gave her peace for a moment.

Her citizens had been so excited to be given the chance to fight and to be offered the opportunity to change how they lived. She knew it would come at great cost. Though the syragons couldn't wield magic, they were far superior in strength.

"You're unsettled." Her husband's voice rumbled from behind her. He stood with his arms crossed, leaning against the post at the end of the bed when she turned around. She smiled at the site if him.

"I'm analyzing the reality of what could happen today. That is all."

"There's no reason to. We will win." Hesitation was not in his tone. He was confident that there was no outcome where they would lose.

"It would be arrogant of you to think there's no possible chance of something taking us by surprise. We're not fighting the most rational or ethical creatures." Luka walked away to get himself ready.

"Did you really just call me arrogant?" He asked from the bathroom.

"It happens to be one of your most well known traits, my dear."

"Well it won you over so it can't be that bad of a trait to have." He smirked, giving her a flirtatious grin as he passed her on his way to the closet.

"It was not your arrogance that won me over. Let me assure you." A chuckle escaped her as she thought back to when they first met. He was intriguing to her, unlike anyone she had ever met before. He was also full of himself, emitting confidence above every other monarch.

"Oh do tell what it really was then, Princess. What is it that won your heart? It was my crown, wasn't it?" He joked.

She rolled her eyes when he called her Princess. She stood and walked over to him as he pulled his thermal shirt on. Her head only reached his chest and his broad shoulders even now made her feel protected.

"Your authenticity." She stated. "You didn't act like something you weren't. You have always been true to who you are. Not to mention you have an uncanny ability to get things done when others are simply all talk." She reached for his hand. He was staring down at her with a smile. "And you protected me. In front of others, from others...You were the only person that could make me feel safe when I was busy trying to protect everyone else."

"I will always protect you Alveen." He wrapped his arms around her. Instantly she felt a wave of clarity and calm roll over her. No one else could make her feel that. "Now that that is settled, are you ready to check on your army?"

"Whenever you are." She stood waiting as he pulled his boots on. She thought for a moment how the man before her embraced her independence and strength and about how they were a team. She didn't overshadow him in her reign and he didn't try to act as though he were more important than her. They supported each other's decisions, sometimes through a long debate, but they always had each other's back. A small smile creeped across her lips as they walked out of the room flanked by guards.

The village was buzzing already. The suns had yet to rise in the star filled sky. If they weren't preparing for a battle that could surely cause many to lose their lives, perhaps Banri Alveen would have enjoyed a moment of its beauty, but her mind was elsewhere. Her boots rhythmically stepped on the cobblestone street as she approached the training grounds with Luka on her side. Only a few of her army were training. She assumed many were still with their families, trying to spend as much time with them as they could.

Sir Caspian was talking with his generals in the armory, ensuring communication was clear and the strategy was well understood.

"Your Majesties." They all knelt before the reigning couple. "We are prepared. Alicorns are prepped and saddled. Bulgrakta's machine techs have looked over their transportation as well. Many are simply awaiting the order to leave."

"I'm pleased to hear this." King Luka spoke. "We best be moving soon. There's no point in standing around waiting when we have other armys to meet."

"I agree, give the word. We're off the ground within the hour." Banri Alveen stated. Both of the royals began to lead the alicorns to the field where they could lift off without issue. Their armies were already smaller than usual to ensure that both Cosaint and Bulgrakta still had forces protecting their borders. Half of the remaining army would travel by Bulgraktan train, arriving hours before the others who would fly in on alicorn.

"Remember. We come in on the mountain top just north of Irielle. Krumvite will be coming in from the sea and up the river so we must have access and Loxley will travel by air as well. We are the first wave, we must ensure a perimeter is set for all of those coming in after." Sir Caspian spoke loudly to the army waiting to depart. Soldiers still trickled in as he spoke which would normally be grounds for serious discipline but given the circumstances of them trying to spend one last moment with their families, Caspian didn't pursue it. "I expect those falling behind this morning to look to your neighbor and guarantee you understand what will be happening."

At the lead, Caspian unfolded the wings on his armor and charged through the field with determination until his mechanism caught the wind and lifted him into the air. The soldiers of the second wave followed. The first wave soldiers traveled with Luka given the Bulgraktan transportation was far superior in speed. Alveen led the third wave on a longer route in order to separate the army in the event that they were lying in wait somewhere.

Luka and Alveen exchanged a loving glance but refused to let their emotions get carried away. They would see each other on the other side, they would both make it out of this war alive.

The Bulgraktan train's whistle echoed through the mountains. Luka closed the door with Ruslan and Tanilly in his wave, and they disappeared into the darkness of the early morning sky. Alveen was left with her wave of soldiers. Stella and Griffith traveled with her. Her heart wasn't beating fast, if anything it felt slower than normal. This was where she belonged. Leading. She closed her eyes for a moment sitting atop of Allicent. The breeze rushing up from the south mountains blew her loose hair over her shoulder. Inhaling deeply, she calmed the restless magic inside of her. Through her minimal time alone she had learned more of the connection between the elements and the magic elves were born with. She could use it to calm or ignite the magic within her. With one last look towards the palace, she saw the few people she trusted to protect her kingdom standing near the ramp. Magnus and Killian among them. Confidence and faith were the only feelings she had when she finally looked away. With a loud yell of encouragement in the native tongue she pushed forward, holding her staff high above her head, and lifted into the now dimly lit sky with part of her army in tow.

The sun rose and reflected hues of orange, gold and purple off of the sea below them. She slid her staff into a slot on her leather saddle for the time being. Alveen occasionally reached out with her magic to sense how everyone was feeling. Some were worried and anxious, so she calmed them. Some were excited, others ready for this battle to be over. It was a full days flight requiring them to stop on a large island to rest and eat. It was documented on their maps and seemed to be plenty large enough to serve their purpose. It was still hours before they would reach it.

"Your Majesty!" One of the guards shrieked. Spears burst through the water shooting into the sky, only narrowly missing them.

"Scatter! Rendezvous on the island!" She ordered. A centaur was hit, thankfully the Loxlian armor he wore didn't allow for it to penetrate but it knocked the wind out of him, keeping him from breathing properly. "Allicent!" She nudged him with her heel and dove after her soldier, keeping her eyes on the sea below her. Another soldier on alicorn dove alongside her, both of them catching an arm of the centaur. They spun around and flew high into the sky to get a better look at the ambush. Her army had scattered, no bodies had fallen into the water from what she could see.

"Let's go." She demanded. The flight to the island was awkward as the alicorns had to pace with one another and avoid each other's wings. "Do you know his name?" She asked.

"Tamarius." She took her other hand off the reins.

"Keep it steady Allcient." She summoned the wind around them, pushing for it to squeeze between the breastplate and Tamarius's chest. With a forceful push, the manipulated air undented the armor. "Tamarius? Can you hear us? I need you to take a slow deep breath." Tamarius was nearly unconscious, but he managed slow shallow breaths. The armor had kept his lungs from expanding and kept him from being able to breath in. "Okay, we need to get to the island. He needs medical attention. Thankfully he can at least breathe now. He can hold out." She looked to the soldier that had flown to her aid. "What's your name soldier?"

"Landen, Your Majesty."

"Thank-you, Landen."

The island was on the horizon and they could see small fires. Relief washed over her as she saw a small portion of her army settling in.

"Medical! Is our doctor here yet?" Alveen yelled as they slowly landed on the beach. Each group had left with multiple medical personnel. They gently laid Tamarius by the first fire they came to. A young witch ran out from the trees to Tamarius's side. Alveen quickly explained the injury before stepping back and evaluating. She turned to one of the soldiers. "How many have arrived?"

"Over half are here already, Your Majesty. It looks like more are arriving." She extended her arm to show Alveen the silhouettes of a large group coming in for landing.

"Your name?"

"Alani."

"Please collect the supply bags and ensure everyone eats." She nodded and turned away, beginning to collect the bags and distribute food. "Landon?" She motioned for him.

"Yes, Your Majesty?""

"Will you please look over the Alicorns for injury? Grab others to help you if you need. We still have flying to do. I want all injuries looked at before we leave." He bowed and walked away, calling for others to join him. Alveen looked over her people. They looked tired, but not shaken or harmed. Once again, she reached out her magic to get a read on the emotions of them. Overall morale seemed nearly unmoved from earlier. She should have guessed. Cosaintian soldiers were strong of body and mind. Walking to the water's edge she let out a long high pitched whistle, the one the mermaids taught her not long after she first arrived. She paced by the closest fire until small smooth heads emerged from the water.

"Shaya. It's so nice to see you my friend." She spoke as she walked to the water.

"Likewise, Queen Alveen. We've heard many wonderful things about your leadership."

"I'm happy to hear this" she paused only for a second, "Will you do me a favor?" She asked, not wanting to waste time. She trusted the mermaids. They were loyal allies to her personally.

"Of course. As you have always been there for us to call on, we would happily do the same." Shaya's barren black eyes stared at her, anxiously awaiting.

"There are some syragons still underwater. We were attacked on our flight here. Will you travel to Krumvite and inform King Viktor? And send others to the unmarked islands? More of my people are there, they need to know to be prepared." Shaya smiled and swung her tail.

"Of course. We will move with haste. We have not seen Syragons on our travels. Normally their stench is everywhere."

"It was quite a way from here. Thankfully we have only had a few injuries, but no casualties. I know your speed is unmatched underwater. I appreciate this." With a nod and a fist over her heart, something she had learned from Caspian, she flipped out of the water and swam away, whistling for others to join her. After being joined, the pod of mermaids broke off and swam in different directions.

The fire warmed her cheeks and hands that the night air had chilled. A few tents were staked in place, but Alveen chose to lay by the fire with Allicent next to her.

"Everyone is accounted for, My Queen." Alani spoke as she sat near her around the fire.

"Your work is appreciated. Thank you for doing all of that." She stared into the fire, feeling herself fall asleep. "You best get some rest, we need to leave in only a few hours."

They rose with the sun and quickly, without disturbance, reached the perimeter of the mountain top. Luka and his personal guard stood in the clearing waiting. He looked composed but his eyes searched her and Allicent for injury, then flickered to the remainder of the group.

"Sirena told us last night. What happened?" He asked as he wrapped her in a hug. Siena was another in Shaya's pod. He led her to the fire after she petted Allicent and allowed the guards to attend to him. She told him about the attack.

"It was sudden but, thankfully our worst injury was Tamarius, who is up and flying again. We have Loxlian armor to thank for that."

"Katherine's soldiers arrived late last night. Viktor's early this morning. You were the last."

"Aw, were you worried for me King Luka?" She nudged him.

"Never. I have more confidence in you alone than any other person I have ever met." They sat in silence for some time while Alveen's wave of soldiers were looked over and fed again.

"Queen Alveen. Happy to see you are unharmed. These Dorcha are not making this world peace thing easy, are they?" King Viktor sat across the fire, wrapped in a thick jacket.

"Nice to see you, Viktor. How's Willow? Not able to sit still I'm sure?"

"You guess correctly. She's back in Foresi for a short time. Hopefully hunting and shooting things will help ease her mind." He chuckled thinking of his wife.

The Generals lined up the alicorns and called upon the troops. Caspian approached them. "We're ready, Your Majesties." With a deep breath, they all stood and walked to their alicorns, riding to the front of the army, ready to lead them to what would hopefully be the final battlefield.

• • •

There was no other way to end this war. The leader of the Dorcha would always be replaced by another with a lust for nothing but blood. Unless they fought and took on the tribe as a whole, there was no other option. The five remaining kingdoms stood together, united against a greater evil. Though their cultures were vastly different, they had always worked so well together. They appreciated and respected their differences, even when they made solutions difficult. In this war, they would each use their own strategies and working together, they would overcome and provide a new legacy for the next line of monarchs.

Alveen's heightened vision could see the look of betrayal on her brother's face. He had actually thought she would give up everything she was responsible for and loved, just to follow him down a path she didn't believe in. He had become someone she no longer recognized. He had become someone that followed the masses and did what others told him was best. Alveen had never been that way, risking her reputation to do what she believed to be right even if others didn't approve. They had become so different since arriving here. Or maybe they were that different all along. Luka looked into her eyes, sitting atop Beastil. He wanted to ask if she was sure she should do this, but he knew his wife. He knew she was strong enough to overcome the emotional battle she would face before the physical one even took place. He admired her strength and how she set a strong example.

"Let's end this." Alveen said, raising her staff into the air. She took one final look at Tanilly, perched in the woods nearby with her guards. Her magic had become so controlled that she was their secret weapon. Tanilly wanted to fight and from a distance, Alveen had no problem with that since she had more power in her right hand then all the citizens in Cosaint.

Charging forward the alicorns took flight, racing towards their enemies. Roaring rumbled the air as the remaining Dorcha members and syragons charged. The suspense built with every gallop towards her brother.

A white light pulsed in the center of the field, throwing her off guard. Luka saw it too. Then another, a small orb grew larger and larger, pulsing with magic. Alveen could feel it calling to her.

"Halt!" She called to her citizens. The royals repeated her order. They had no idea what this was and the last thing she wanted to do was send her citizens and warriors into an unknown ball of energy. The Dorcha still charged. "How are they doing this?" She asked Caspian to her left.

"I don't believe this is them, Your Grace." as the front line of their opponents reached the orb, the ground shook and a ripple of energy was sent out from the orb, dismounting every warrior and sending both Solas and Dorcha tribe members onto their backs. Alveen held up her staff, healing those she could feel were wounded and bringing others to their feet.

As they gathered to watch this phenomenon occur right on their battlefield, the orb opened much like a portal. Through this new dimensional door marched elves. Dozens of elves on top of oversized wolves, bears, snow leopards and mountain lions.

These were the elves they had seen when they tried traveling to the first world. They had been rerouted to their world, unable to communicate.

"This has taken a very odd turn." Luka spoke. Everyone watched at the newcomers lined strategically. Alveen stared with her heightened senses at the commander of this new group. Was he friend or foe to them? She couldn't tell.

Alveen mounted Allicent and walked forward with her staff. The leader approached her as well. Center field, they stood silent. This new group, though they looked like elves, were far larger than any species on Beannithe. Their eyes, she could see now, were many colors. Their bodies, lean and strong. The oversized wolf towered over Allicent, making him nervous. Luka walked up to her side.

"Welcome. I am Queen Alveen of Cosaint and Bulgrakta."

"And I am King Luka of Cosaint and Bulgrakta. We ask who you are and your intentions in our world?" Luka was straight forward. Though it didn't help since they didn't speak the same language. The leaders response seemed purposeful. They came here for something, but they couldn't understand.

"Um, Aunt Alveen?" Tanilly spoke. The young girl had left her post in the nearby woods and walked to the field.

"Tanilly! What are you doing here?" Her maternal side wanted to express how dangerous this was, but they had crossed that line when they accepted the fact that she was one of their strongest warriors and assets. The young girl just smiled, but her face gave way to more emotion than that.

"No, Alveen. They won't hurt me." She stated, still staring at the leader. His eyes grew and he let out a gasp.

"You don't know that." Alveen answered, worried how this situation would progress.

"I do. I also know why I have so many more powers than all of you." She finally looked away from the commander of the group. "I am them. This is my father."

Alveen and Luka both stayed silent, confusion taking them by surprise. Tanilly spoke the language of the leader.

"Tanilly this isn't possible. You are part fairy." She translated, surprising everyone with her new found ability to speak and unknown language. The commander of the newcomers spoke.

"But I'm not. My blood tests even proved, there is no fairy in my veins. I'm rare."

The conversation went back and forth for a while before the oversized, war paint covered commander lifted her in his arms with a relieved expression.

"Tanilly? What happened? How did this happen?" Luka was finally able to ask. She smiled and translated for her father back to them.

"When I was born, I was taken from them. They have looked everywhere for me and my captures. They know it wasn't you, but they were not able to travel here until you guys opened the portal there and left the trail for them to follow.

"So you *are* a totally different species. Just like the blood test said. Not evolved."

"Yep. It sounds like there was a small group of elves who broke off this tribe and created life in this new world." Tanilly explained as her father spoke.

"The original monarchs." Luka and Alveen said in unison. "Tanilly, who kidnapped you?" Her eyebrows furrowed. She pointed toward Zakarian and Malika, who they could now see were trying to flee the battle.

The commander yelled something in a harsh tone, sending a group of his warriors towards the Dorcha. Hands held out to the sides, nearly touching each other as they rode atop their beasts, they created a magic force field and sent it flying forward. Within seconds, the entire Dorcha tribe was incinerated. All but Zakarian and Malika, who were brought back to The Commander. He set down Tanilly and said a few words to her, making her turn around. Before their eyes, The Commander grabbed each of them and ripped their bodies in half. The tribe behind him began to holler and cheer with triumph. Their bodies tossed to his wolf and a nearby

● ● ●

mountain lion. Alveen froze, feeling the sting of watching her brother murdered. She had decided when she declared this battle that his death was needed for this world to see peace again. She even decided that she would cover her emotions and she would be the one to do it. She expected him to die today, but it still took her not so hardened heart by surprise.

"I'm their lost Princess. Queen actually." Tanilly stated looking at her adoptive parents.

Luka and Alveen slowly backed up, glancing at each other. "So what does this mean?" Luka asked. "How do we even know they are telling the truth?" Tanilly spoke to her father again. He smiled, a real smile, at the newlywed royals. He spoke a few words to Tanilly and she translated again.

"First, how else do you explain my understanding this language? Second, I remember. The first pulse of energy from the orb, when it hit me and my memory came back. Even though I was little, I remember their world." Luka and Alveen just stared at each other for a moment.

"It would explain why no one remembers her being pregnant. But Zakarian should have been on Earth then... not here." Alveen analyzed. "Tanilly, this is crazy. You are our family. You cannot simply think we will just let them take you." It was silent for a moment. Tanilly remembered only her few days as an infant, Alveen and Luka had become her parents, even if it wasn't by blood. In her armor, she stood confused and unsure of how this would unfold before her. The commander spoke in their native language.

• • •

"He said if not for the fact that you've protected me all this time, this world would have been wiped out the moment they arrived." Tanilly translated. "But they are willing to negotiate peace with you."

"That is a much more desirable solution than going to battle after seeing what they just did to the Dorcha. Allow us to get our commanders and the other royals in order to begin." Tanilly translated. Her father rolled his eyes and responded. Tanilly translated.

"One of the many differences between our worlds. I alone rule our people, you need a committee to rule yours." He scoffed. Luka and Alveen slowly walked back to their people, the other royals meeting them ahead of their army.

"We are negotiating peace." Luka stated.

"Who are these creatures? Why do we need to negotiate peace? They are in our world." Viktor argued, feeling in the dark and demanding answers.

"Long story short, our original monarchs came from their world. So did Tanilly. And if you didn't happen to see what they are capable of, I believe it is in our best interest to not go to war with them." Alveen tried to summarize for her fellow monarchs. Everyone wore expressions of unease. Though the Dorcha tribes were officially eliminated, it was possible that another, more capable and powerful enemy was now in their presence.

Karolyn spoke up, "Our ancestors split from them. They left that world for a reason. Though they clearly thought it a well enough secret to leave out of our history, there had to be a good reason. Should we really be making peace with a world and species we know nothing about?"

"I understand your concerns as they are mine as well. I believe the only way we leave this field alive is if we come to an agreement with them. The point of a peace treaty is for us to leave each other be. If they do things in their world that we wouldn't do in ours, then we stick to our own world. It is their culture and we have no power there. My main concern is getting us all home safely tonight and giving us a steady foundation with these new possible allies." She whistled and raised her arm, calling for Sir Caspian's attention. The centaur was at her side within moments.

"We should all be there negotiating. We are all monarchs." Viktor stated bluntly.

"If you all wish to be involved in the negotiating, you're welcome to join. We are not excluding anyone." Luka took over talking with the Monarchs as Alveen and Caspian discussed strategy. Caspian was trained in this area and Alveen ·was quick to acknowledge that she had never had experience making peace. Most of her rule had been war and recovery. Karolyn was the only monarch that may have had experience, or heard about the treaties between the Solas kingdoms. There was once feuds and rivalry in Beannithe, but that was at the beginning of their time.

The four monarchs with Sir Caspian at their side, made their way to the towering newcomers on what was supposed to be the battlefield. Smoke rolled in their view as a chilled breeze cut across the field, carrying the ashes of their eliminated enemies. The sun was high in the sky but the air was still cold around them.

As they approached the circle Tanilly came to stand at Queen Alveen's side, lightly touching her forearm. Alveen felt comfort as her adopted daughter approached her. That is, until a sense of urgency washed over her. It took her a moment to tell it was coming from Tanilly. The young girl's face showed calm and collected, but the emotions she was sharing were anything but. A small voice echoed, almost quieter than a whisper, in Alveen's mind.

Don't do it. They aren't to be trusted. You see what they've done already. Their world is full of war and pain and we cannot allow it to purge the world our ancestors died creating.

Alveen had to make a decision with haste. Everyone around her assumed they were creating the guidelines for negotiating peace. Tanilly was the only one that could understand them and had them memories of their world. She held an expression revealing nothing as she responded. They were so close now.

How do you know their world is still like that? Why are they not to be trusted?

Only a moment passed until she heard a response.

Because, I could see it. and feel it. When he hugged me. It was cold and the memories continued to flow in from him. They plan to bring war here. He said so. He thinks we're easy to wipe out and this world will be used as a prison.

If that was even partly true, Alveen had to do her duty as Queen of her own people and take initiative, but how?

What do you recommend?

Follow my lead. Be ready.

Alveen shot Luka a glance that to others may have seemed cold, but he understood to be a warning.

Tanilly introduced the other monarchs to the species that had been revealed as the Archumonds. Caspian declared a usual set of guidelines created for peace treaty's but before while he spoke, Tanilly and Alveen were making a plan. Tanilly had picked up some tricks while digging around in the commander's mind. One thrust, that's all it would take to incinerate them like they had the Dorcha tribe, assuming they

• • •

didn't have something preventing them from being harmed. With focus and all the strength, they could muster, Alveen's arms began to glow as they released the swarm of power that had accumulated inside them. Luka reached for her in an instant, summoning whatever he could from the ground below him. Spears pointed at them but the tips were melted as the burst of magic quickly sped up the metal rods and through the army of newcomers. Bodies turned to ashes, floating away in the wind. The monarchs and Caspian stood dumbfounded as the silence was broken by huffing from Alveen and Tanilly.

"I thought we were negotiating peace!?" Exclaimed King Viktor. Queen Alveen responded with confidence.

"We were. But Tanilly was able to discover disturbing news about their intentions while we made that decision. If I had a way to communicate with you, believe me, I would have."

"What could possibly have been so bad it was worth incinerating them? And how are you able to do exactly what they did?" Queen Karolyn expressed. "You could have done that many times before."

"That was me. When he hugged me I could see his memories, not just my own. I could hear his thoughts. His intentions were world dominating." Tanilly responded quietly. She knew she had no royal position, but she knew what she saw wasn't something she could let happen.

As they walked back, there was cheering from the crowds that had sat back unsure of the direction this would take. Peace would finally fall over all the kingdoms. They could rebuild boarders and replace the barriers that protected each kingdom from the evil that used to sneak between the mountains they lived on.

The monarchs and citizens all returned home unharmed that day and life in Beannithe has been filled with peace ever since. With a blood test it was proven that Rowna of Irielle was actually 70% elven. With practice she was able to control magic and pass her trials, making her Queen of Irielle, which was fitting since she was the only remaining citizen other than the twins. Irielle was cleaned, rebuilt and opened up for citizens to travel to and call their home. Rowna and Karolyn trained the girls. She often reminds them of their mother and heritage from the once strong kingdom.

For years my family has watched over the members of the monarchy. Scratching down every event, every conversation, from the shadows. We blend in. We change appearances as to not give away our constant presence, we even mastered being able to turn transparent in order to get the most details and avoid detection altogether.

It was my great grandmother that followed Queen Alveen around from birth. She took on many forms, even that of animals in order to keep within distance of The Queen. My father followed King Bowen, then upon his death, King Viktor.

I come from a long line of scribes in the shadows. None of these societies know of our existence, and if we continue to do our jobs right, they never will, for our job is simply to document history, the truth of it.

The End.

www.ingramcontent.com/pod-product-compliance
Lightning Source LLC
Chambersburg PA
CBHW030820020726
47499CB00006B/2003